Kokoro

Kokoro
Natsume Sōseki

MINT EDITIONS

Kokoro was first published in 1914.

This edition published by Mint Editions 2021.

ISBN 9781513283296 | E-ISBN 9781513288314

Published by Mint Editions®

minteditionbooks.com

Publishing Director: Jennifer Newens
Design & Production: Rachel Lopez Metzger
Project Manager: Micaela Clark
Typesetting: Westchester Publishing Services

Contents

Book One. Sensei and I

Chapter 1	13
Chapter 2	15
Chapter 3	17
Chapter 4	19
Chapter 5	21
Chapter 6	23
Chapter 7	25
Chapter 8	27
Chapter 9	29
Chapter 10	31
Chapter 11	33
Chapter 12	35
Chapter 13	37
Chapter 14	39
Chapter 15	41
Chapter 16	43
Chapter 17	45

CHAPTER 18	47
CHAPTER 19	49
CHAPTER 20	51
CHAPTER 21	53
CHAPTER 22	55
CHAPTER 23	57
CHAPTER 24	59
CHAPTER 25	61
CHAPTER 26	63
CHAPTER 27	65
CHAPTER 28	67
CHAPTER 29	69
CHAPTER 30	71
CHAPTER 31	73
CHAPTER 32	75
CHAPTER 33	77
CHAPTER 34	79
CHAPTER 35	81
CHAPTER 36	83

Book Two. My Parents and I

Chapter 1	87
Chapter 2	89
Chapter 3	91
Chapter 4	93
Chapter 5	95
Chapter 6	97
Chapter 7	99
Chapter 8	101
Chapter 9	103
Chapter 10	105
Chapter 11	107
Chapter 12	109
Chapter 13	111
Chapter 14	113
Chapter 15	115
Chapter 16	117
Chapter 17	119
Chapter 18	121

Book Three. Sensei's Testament

Chapter 1	125
Chapter 2	127
Chapter 3	129
Chapter 4	131
Chapter 5	133
Chapter 6	135
Chapter 7	137
Chapter 8	139
Chapter 9	141
Chapter 10	143
Chapter 11	145
Chapter 12	147
Chapter 13	149
Chapter 14	151
Chapter 15	153
Chapter 16	155
Chapter 17	157
Chapter 18	159
Chapter 19	161

Chapter 20	163
Chapter 21	165
Chapter 22	167
Chapter 23	169
Chapter 24	171
Chapter 25	173
Chapter 26	175
Chapter 27	177
Chapter 28	179
Chapter 29	181
Chapter 30	183
Chapter 31	185
Chapter 32	187
Chapter 33	189
Chapter 34	191
Chapter 35	193
Chapter 36	195
Chapter 37	197
Chapter 38	199
Chapter 39	201

Chapter 40	203
Chapter 41	205
Chapter 42	207
Chapter 43	209
Chapter 44	211
Chapter 45	213
Chapter 46	215
Chapter 47	217
Chapter 48	219
Chapter 49	221
Chapter 50	223
Chapter 51	225
Chapter 52	227
Chapter 53	229
Chapter 54	231
Chapter 55	233
Chapter 56	235

BOOK ONE
SENSEI AND I

Chapter 1

I always called him Sensei. Herein, therefore, I will write of him as Sensei and not use his true name. It's not so much that I fear how the world may judge him, but rather that it feels to me more natural. Whenever I think of him, the word "Sensei" immediately forms on my lips. As I take up my pen, the same feeling arises. To use an initial, or some such detached term, would be to make him a stranger.

It was in Kamakura that I first met Sensei. I was a student then, still in my youth. I'd received a postcard from a friend who was at the seaside for the summer. He invited me to come join him, so I scraped together some money and departed. It took me several days to secure my funds. Then, not three days after my arrival in Kamakura, the friend who'd invited me was suddenly summoned home by telegram. According to the telegram, his mother was ill. My friend, however, doubted this. He'd been pressured for some time, by his parents back home in the country, toward a marriage match in which he took little interest. In this modern day, he was too young for marriage. On top of this, the all-important other party was not to his liking. This was why he was summering outside of Tōkyō, instead of returning home as usual. He showed me the telegram and asked my advice. I didn't know what to tell him, other than that if his mother really were ill then he must, by all means, go to her. In the end, he decided to go. As a result, I was left on my own.

The start of classes was still a long way off. I could stay in Kamakura or I could go back—the decision was mine. I decided to stay put, at least for the time being. My friend was of a wealthy family in the Chūgoku region, and he was never wanting for money. Nevertheless, he was a student like myself, and young like myself, so our styles of living were not dissimilar. Accordingly, I could remain on my own there without the trouble of seeking a lesser room.

My inn was in a remote quarter of Kamakura. Playing billiards, eating ice cream, or other such fashionable engagements, required a long walk through the fields. Rickshaws were available, but the fare was twenty sen. Nevertheless, there were a number of private villas scattered here and there. The sea was close by, so the situation, for bathers, was quite ideal.

Every day I set out for the sea. As I made my way past old, soot-darkened thatch roofs and descended toward the beach, I would wonder at the multitude of city dwellers residing here to escape the heat. Atop the sand was a mass of men and women in motion. At times, the sea itself was packed with dark heads, much like a bath house. I knew not a soul among them. Amidst by this vibrant scene, I enjoyed myself immensely, lazing on the sand, breaking the waves with my knees, or jumping about in the surf.

It was within this throng that I first spotted Sensei. At that time, there were two beach-side tea huts. I had come, by happenstance, to frequent one of the two. Unlike those in the grand villas of Hase, the vacationers here did not have access to dedicated facilities and were reliant on shared changing rooms. At the tea huts, in addition to relaxing over tea, guests could launder their bathing suits, wash the salt from their bodies, and check personal items such as hats or parasols. I didn't own a bathing suit, but I was concerned for my belongings, so before swimming I would check them all at the tea hut.

Chapter 2

When I first saw Sensei at the beach-side tea hut, he was just disrobing in preparation for a swim. I, myself, was doing the reverse, having just returned from the water, the breeze cooling my wet body. There were numerous dark heads in motion between us, obstructing our line of sight. Under normal circumstances I would never have noticed Sensei. However, in spite of the crowd, and in spite of my own wandering mind, I did notice him. The reason I did was a Westerner in his company.

The skin of this Westerner was conspicuously fair, and it caught my attention as soon as I entered the tea hut. He'd been dressed in an authentic Japanese yukata, which he'd dropped neatly onto his stool. He then stood there with arms folded, surveying the sea. He wore his undershorts, the same kind we wore, and nothing else. This struck me as curious. Two days before I'd ventured to Yuigahama. I'd crouched on the sand for a long while and watched the Westerners bathe. My spot was slightly elevated and close to the hotel's rear entrance. As I'd crouched there, numerous men had emerged and headed for the surf. All had covered torsos, covered thighs, and covered arms. The ladies concealed their flesh even more so. Most wore rubber swim caps of maroon, navy, or indigo that bobbed distinctly in the waves. After witnessing such a scene, this Westerner standing here before us, in nothing but his undershorts, was truly novel.

He finally turned round and spoke a few words to a Japanese man who was stooping nearby. The Japanese man was picking up a towel that had fallen in the sand. As soon as he had it, he tied it around his head and proceeded toward the sea. This man was Sensei.

Out of sheer curiosity, I watched as the two of them walked, side by side, down to the water. I watched them proceed directly into the surf. They traversed the shallows, passing through throngs of boisterous bathers, reached a relatively deserted space, and began to swim. They swam toward the open sea, and I watched as their heads grew smaller. Then they turned and made a bee line back to the shore. Again in the tea hut, they wiped themselves dry without rinsing, dressed, and promptly departed.

After they left, I went back to my stool, sat down, and had a smoke. As I smoked, my mind, somewhat vacantly, wandered back to Sensei.

I couldn't help but think that I'd seen him somewhere before. Try as I might, though, I failed to place him.

By that time, rather than carefree pleasure, I was feeling a sense of tedium. The next day, I took it upon myself to return to the tea hut again at the same hour. The Westerner did not show, but Sensei arrived, wearing a straw hat. He placed his glasses on the table, tied his towel around his head, and walked briskly down to the water's edge. Just like the day before, he cut past the boisterous bathers and began to swim out alone. As he did so, I was seized with the urge to follow. Kicking up water as I splashed through the shallows, I proceeded out to the depths. Once there, I began to swim arm over arm toward Sensei. Unlike the prior day, however, Sensei cut back toward the shore in an unexpected arc. Thwarted in my effort, I failed to catch him. When I came up from the water and entered the tea hut, still shaking the drops from my hands, Sensei had already dressed. We met in passing as he made his way out.

Chapter 3

The following day I was back at the beach at the same time, and again I saw Sensei. The day after that, I repeated the same routine. No opportunity arose, though, for greeting or exchange of words. Sensei's demeanor, in fact, was very much aloof. He arrived and departed like clockwork, all the while in a world of his own. However lively the scene around him might be, he appeared to pay it no mind. The Westerner, who was there the first time, did not return. Sensei was always alone.

On one occasion, Sensei walked up from the sea in his signature brisk manner, grabbed the yukata he'd tossed aside in the usual place, and found that, for whatever reason, there was a good deal of sand on its surface. He turned around and shook it several times. As he did so his glasses, which he'd placed beneath the garment, slipped between the planks and fell to the ground. Sensei donned his yukata, which was white with splashed accents, and tied his waist cord. Then he noticed his glasses were missing and immediately began to search. I ducked my head under the bench and picked up the glasses. Sensei thanked me as he took them from my hand.

On the next day, I followed Sensei into the surf. I swam out after him in the same direction. About two hundred meters out, Sensei turned back and greeted me. The two of us were alone out there, floating on a wide blue canvas of open sea. Intense sunlight bathed the sea and surrounding hills for as far as the eye could reach. I splashed about in the open water, a feeling of freedom and joy coursing through every muscle. Sensei, for his part, suddenly ceased all motion and rested on his back on the waves. I followed suit. The blue of the sky rained down in intense color, dazzling my eyes. "It's wonderful here," I called out.

After a while Sensei, as though waking in the middle of the sea, righted himself. "Shall we head back?" he suggested. Not lacking for stamina, my preference was to remain longer and enjoy the sea. However, at Sensei's suggestion I readily acquiesced. Together, we retraced our path and returned to the shore.

This was the start of my friendship with Sensei. I still didn't know, though, where he was staying.

Several more days passed, and I believe it was the afternoon of the third day. When I saw Sensei at the tea house, he turned to me and asked, out of the blue, if I intended to stay a good while longer. With no specific plans, I was ill prepared to answer his question. "I'm not really sure," was all I could manage. When I saw the grin on Sensei's face, I grew somewhat abashed. "And yourself, Sensei?" I felt compelled to ask in return. This was the first time I addressed him as Sensei.

That evening, I called on Sensei at his lodgings. He was not at a typical inn, but rather in a villa-like structure that was built on the vast grounds of a temple. I learned that he was staying as a guest there, having no family connection to the site. Each time I addressed him as Sensei, it seemed to elicit a forced smile. I had to explain that such was the way I always addressed my elders. I asked about the foreigner from the other day. Sensei talked of him for a bit, telling me, among other things, of his eccentricity and of how he had already left Kamakura. Sensei then added that, given his limited fellowship with his own countrymen, it was curious that he'd made the acquaintance of a foreigner. At the end of the evening, I turned to Sensei and divulged that I thought I knew him from somewhere, but couldn't say where. Young and hopeful, I expected that Sensei should harbor a similar feeling. I eagerly awaited his answer. Sensei, for his part, pondered in silence for a moment and then replied, "You don't look at all familiar. It must have been someone else." My anticipation gave way to disappointment.

Chapter 4

I returned to Tōkyō at the end of the month. Sensei had vacated his own summer place a good while earlier. On parting from Sensei, I'd asked if I might call on him from time to time. In a curt manner, he replied merely that, yes, I was welcome to stop by. I felt we'd developed a strong bond, and I'd expected something a little more heartfelt. His tepid response took my confidence down a notch.

In many such cases, I met with mild disappointment. It's possible that Sensei was aware of this, or it could be he had no idea. Through all these minor disappointments, I was never inclined to end our association. On the contrary, in fact, each brush with insecurity drew me further along. Up ahead, I believed, whatever it was I hoped for would appear before my eyes, and all would be right. I was in my youth. However, I was not inclined to expend my youthful energy on just anyone. I didn't know what it was, but something about Sensei warranted my engagement. Now at last, after Sensei's passing, I've begun to understand. From the very start, Sensei never disliked me. His occasional curt reply or cool demeanor were neither expressions of displeasure nor intent to drive me away. Sensei, wretched in his own being, was wont to hold others at arm's length. Believing himself unworthy, he fended off all who approached too near. Sensei's aversion to intimacy, rather than rising from disdain for others, was rooted in disdain for himself.

When I returned to Tōkyō, I had every intention of calling on Sensei. There were still two weeks before the start of classes, and I thought to go once in the interim. After being back for a few days, though, those feelings from Kamakura began to fade. The mood of the vibrant city, and the excitement of re-engaging in its rhythms, fully occupied my mind. As I saw the streets full of students, I felt anew the aspirations and apprehensions of a coming school year. For a while, I thought no further of Sensei.

After a month of classes, I was starting to feel drained. I walked the streets with a certain air of displeasure. In my room, my gaze wandered wistfully from one thing to another. Visions of Sensei came to mind. I wanted to see him again.

The first time I called at his home, Sensei was away. The second time, as I remember it, was the following Sunday. It was wonderful weather, the kind of day where the clear sky cleanses the soul. This time, too, Sensei was away. In Kamakura, Sensei had told me himself that he seldom went out. He'd even described himself as reclusive. Having failed twice now to see him, I recalled these words, and I was seized with a vague feeling of discontent. I lingered in the entryway, looking with some hesitation at the maidservant. The maidservant, who had taken my card on the previous occasion, bid me to wait and went back inside. A woman, presumably the lady of the house, appeared in her place. She was quite beautiful.

She kindly informed me of Sensei's whereabouts. Every month, she told me, he visited the cemetery in Zōshigaya to place flowers at the grave of a certain departed soul. "He just left, not ten minutes ago," she said with a look of sympathy. I thanked her and stepped back outside. After walking a block toward the center of town, I decided I should stroll through Zōshigaya. Part of my thinking was that I might see Sensei. I turned on my heels and set off in the new direction.

Chapter 5

I entered to the left through a nursery that fronted the cemetery, traversing a lane with maples planted down both sides. From a tea house at the end of the lane, a man resembling Sensei emerged. I moved nearer, close enough to see the sun reflect off the rims of his glasses. Without further hesitation, I called out, "Sensei!" in a loud voice. Sensei stopped in his tracks and turned my way.

"How did. . . ? How did. . . ?"

Sensei repeated these words twice over. Their tone, as he repeated them, rung heavy in the midday calm. I found myself at a loss for an answer.

"Did you follow me here? How did. . . ?" Sensei's demeanor was perfectly relaxed, and his voice was perfectly restrained. However, a shadow of some sort seemed to pass over his countenance.

I explained to him how I'd come to be there.

"Did my wife tell you whose grave I came to visit?"

"No, that she didn't say."

"I see.—I expect she wouldn't, having only just met you. There's no reason she should."

Sensei seemed finally assured. The meaning of this all eluded me.

On our way back out to the boulevard, Sensei and I passed among the grave sites. There were graves marked 'Isabella so-and-so' and 'Login, Servant of the Lord.' Nearby stood a grave post inscribed with 'All Living Creatures are Endowed with the Essence of Buddha.' Another grave read 'Minister Plenipotentiary so-and-so.' I stopped in front of a small post engraved with 'An Toku Retsu' and asked Sensei about the reading of the characters. "They intended, I suppose, that we read those as André," he replied with a wry smile.

Sensei, it seemed, did not share my interest in these diverse grave markers and the irony of their mutual proximity. I pointed out a round grave stone here, or a column of engraved granite there, and offered my opinion on all. Sensei listened patiently for a while, then finally said, "You've never thought seriously of the reality of death, have you?" I fell silent. Sensei said nothing further.

At the edge of the cemetery stood a single large gingko tree whose vast canopy blotted out the sky. When we were underneath, Sensei looked up into its high branches. "It'll be beautiful here. In a short while the leaves will turn and fall to the ground, carpeting it with gold." Once each month, Sensei passed beneath this tree.

In the distance, a man was smoothing the ground for new grave sites. He rested his hoe and looked our way.

We proceeded on and turned to the left, emerging onto the main thoroughfare.

Having no particular place to go, I simply followed along with Sensei. He was more taciturn than usual. His silence didn't put me off, though, so I ambled comfortably at his side.

"Are you headed home now?"

"Yes. I've no other particular errands."

"Is your family grave site there?" I broke the silence again.

"No."

"Whose grave is it, then?—a relation of yours?"

"No."

Sensei gave no further response, and I stopped questioning. After we'd walked a bit, he abruptly came back to the subject. "The grave is that of a friend."

"You visit your friend's grave once each month?"

"Yes, I do."

Chapter 6

After that, I called at Sensei's house from time to time. I always found him at home. As my visits grew in number, so too did their frequency.

Sensei's manner toward me though, even later on in our friendship, showed little change from the time of our initial encounter. He was always reserved. Sometimes he was too reserved, almost withdrawn. I'd sensed from the start that he was somehow a hard man to approach. At the same time, I'd felt most keenly a need to approach him. I was perhaps, in all the world, the only soul who felt this way toward Sensei. However, this instinct of mine was later vindicated by the course of events. It's a source of both pride and comfort to me now that, despite being deemed naïve or foolish, I trusted my inner voice. A man capable of love, in fact incapable of not loving, yet unable to embrace those whom he would cherish—such a man was Sensei.

As I've mentioned, Sensei was always reserved. He was always composed. However, a peculiar shadow would at times cross his countenance, like the dark shadow of a bird as it passes a window. Almost before one noticed, it was gone again. It was at the cemetery in Zōshigaya, when I'd called out abruptly to Sensei, that I first observed this shadow on his brow. In that brief, unnatural moment, the ebb of my heart had lost a touch of its usual verve. It was just a momentary lapse, and soon enough I was fully myself again. I thought no more on that dark shadow till one evening in late autumn, when suddenly it came back to bear.

I WAS TALKING WITH SENSEI, and in my mind I suddenly pictured the large gingko tree he had pointed out to me. Sensei's monthly visit to the cemetery, I reckoned, should be three days hence. My schedule was light that day, with classes concluding by noon. I turned to Sensei and asked, "Do you think that gingko in Zōshigaya has lost its leaves?"

"I expect it won't be fully bare just yet." Sensei looked me in the eye as he answered. For a moment, he didn't divert his gaze.

I continued. "Next time you go, may I accompany you? We can stroll the grounds together."

"I go to pay my respects. I don't go to stroll."

"But isn't it perfect for strolling as well?"

Sensei gave no reply. After a pause, he added, "No, I go in earnest to pay my respects." He seemed intent on separating his visitation from the idea of a stroll. Perhaps it was just a pretext for going without me. His behavior at the time struck me as eccentric, even childish. I wanted to press the matter. "We'll make it a visitation then. Take me with you. I can pay my respects as well."

To me, a visitation and a stroll were more or less one and the same. At this point, Sensei's brow darkened. A strange light shone in his eyes. He seemed beset by some ill-defined unease. One could distill it down to neither annoyance, nor contempt, nor fear. The memory of that moment in Zōshigaya, when I'd called out to him, came back to me in a flash. The look on his face was exactly the same.

"There are reasons. . ." Sensei started. "There are reasons that I can't explain to you. My visits must be my own. Even my wife never comes with me."

Chapter 7

I thought this peculiar. However, I was not there to scrutinize Sensei, so I simply let it pass. As I look back now, the approach I took toward Sensei is a point of pride. I believe it instilled our relationship with warmth and humanity. Had I probed in the least at Sensei's psyche, had I sought to analyze him, the bond of fellowship between us would have snapped then and there. I was young, of course, and not at all conscious of my own comportment. Perhaps that renders it all the more praiseworthy. I shudder to think of all that I could have done wrong, and of all that would have been lost. Even as things played out, Sensei stayed ever vigilant, even anxiously so, with respect to his privacy.

I came to visit Sensei regularly. I was at his door two or three times each month. One day, when my visits had come to be frequent, Sensei suddenly turned and asked me, "What draws you so often to visit a man like me?"

"What draws me? I can't say it's anything in particular.—Do I impose on you?"

"I didn't say you impose."

Indeed, there was no indication from Sensei that I was unwelcome. I was aware that Sensei kept very limited company. I knew that of his former classmates, two or three at most resided in Tōkyō. Once in a while I shared the parlor with students from Sensei's home region, but it was clear to me that none were as close to him as I was.

"I'm a lonely man," Sensei confided. "That's why I appreciate your visits, and that's why I wonder what draws you here so often."

"But why should you need to ask?"

Sensei didn't answer the question I posed in return. Instead he looked at me and asked, "How old are you?"

To me, the dialogue that followed seemed unrelated to the subject at hand. For the moment, though, I left it at that and pushed no further. However, within four days I was back at Sensei's door.

Sensei smiled as soon as he entered the parlor. "Back already, are you?"

"Yes, I'm back."

Such a welcome, from anyone else, would have left me offended. Coming from Sensei, though, the effect was reversed. Far from feeling offense, I felt delight.

"I'm a lonely man." That evening, Sensei again spoke these same words. "I'm a lonely man, and I wonder if you aren't lonely too. I'm on in years and set in my ways. Your situation is different. Youth has a need to test itself. You'll want to make your mark somewhere. . ."

"I'm not at all lonely."

"There's nothing so lonely as youth. If you aren't lonely, then what draws you here so often?" Sensei repeated these same words yet again. "My company, I'm afraid, will not relieve your loneliness. I don't have the power to grab it for you and pull it out by the roots. You'll have to reach out to others, and once you do, you'll be done with me." Sensei ended with a wistful smile.

Chapter 8

Sensei's prognosis, happily, did not come to pass. But within his prognosis was a clear message that, at the time, lacking in experience, I failed to grasp. I continued my visits. Before long, as a matter of course, I was joining Sensei for dinner. This necessitated, naturally, that I converse with his wife.

Like any other man, I was not indifferent to women. However, I was young at that time and had little experience forging any real ties with the opposite sex. Possibly on this account, my interest was merely passive—musings over unfamiliar women seen on the street. Sensei's wife, when I'd met her before in the entry hall, had impressed me as quite beautiful. On each subsequent meeting, I was impressed again by her beauty. However, beyond that there was nothing that struck me as noteworthy.

This is not to say that Sensei's wife was dull. It should rather be said that she had no occasion to show me her personal side. I came to regard her as a mere extension of Sensei. She, for her part, graciously received me as a student who called on her husband. Apart from Sensei as a common touch point, there was no connection whatsoever between us. From those early encounters, the only impression that remains with me is the impression of her beauty.

On one occasion Sensei and I drank saké together. Sensei's wife joined to serve us. Sensei seemed in unusually good spirits. "You have one too," he said, draining his cup and handing it to his wife. She received it reluctantly, and not without some protest. Knitting her fair brows, she lifted the cup, after I'd filled it halfway for her, and put it to her lips. The following exchange then occurred between husband and wife.

"What's the occasion? You never ask me to drink."

"Only because you don't like to drink. But you should try it sometimes. It's good for the soul."

"I'm afraid it only torments mine. You seem quite jovial, though, from a little saké."

"Sometimes it does the trick, but I can't say that's always the case."

"How about tonight?"

"Tonight I'm feeling fine."

"You should drink a little each night."

"No, that won't do."

"Why not try it, if it works to cheer you?"

In Sensei's household were only the couple themselves and a maidservant. It was always quiet when I called.

Never once did I hear the sound of laughter. It often felt as though Sensei and I were the only ones there.

"It would be nice to have children." Sensei's wife turned to me as she said this. I politely echoed her thought, but I did not, in fact, share her sentiment. Having no family of my own yet, I regarded children as an annoyance.

"Shall we take one in?" Sensei asked her.

"Adoption? Oh, I don't know." She turned my way again.

"We'll never have one of our own," Sensei replied.

His wife was silent. "Why is that?" I asked in turn.

"Divine retribution," Sensei said, and laughed aloud.

Chapter 9

To the best of my knowledge, Sensei and his wife were a happy couple. I was not a part of their household, and I wasn't, of course, privy to their intimate dealings. However, there were times when I sat with Sensei and, having need of something, he would call for his wife rather than the maidservant. (His wife's name was Shizu.) "Hey there, Shizu," he would call out, turning toward the partition. There was a gentle sound to his voice. His wife would answer back, and then appear, in a manner most deferential. When we dined together on occasion and she joined us at the table, this bond between them was clearer still.

Sensei would sometimes take his wife to a concert or the theater. As I recall, it was also not unusual for them to take short trips together. I still have a picture postcard from their visit to Hakone. From Nikkō, they sent me a maple leaf by post.

This was the relationship between Sensei and his wife as I saw it at the time. There was but a single exception. One day, I arrived as usual and was about to announce myself from the entry hall, when I heard the sound of voices from the parlor. Rather than normal conversation, they sounded contentious. The parlor in Sensei's house was just off the entry hall, so standing before the partition I could well discern the tones of a quarrel. The raising of a male voice told me one of the parties was Sensei. The other party was more subdued, and I couldn't be sure, but I sensed it was Sensei's wife. She was possibly in tears. I lingered for a time in the entry hall, wondering what had happened, then quickly departed and returned to my lodgings.

A strange unease washed over me. I tried to read but couldn't concentrate. An hour passed, and Sensei appeared below my window and called my name. Surprised, I opened the window. He asked from below if I'd walk with him. I took out my watch, which was still tucked into the folds of my sash, and saw that it was a bit past eight. I was still dressed as for my visit, so I immediately went out front.

Sensei and I drank beer together that night. Sensei was not a heavy drinker. If the first few drinks didn't cheer him, he wasn't one to double down by drinking more.

"It's no use tonight," he said with a forced smile.

"The drink's not helping you?" I asked with some sympathy.

For my part, the earlier incident had been weighing on my mind the entire time, making me anxious. It was akin to a fishbone stuck in one's throat. I would think about speaking to Sensei frankly, then reconsider and decide not to. These inner vacillations, no doubt, presented themselves outwardly as an odd sort of restlessness.

"You seem out of sorts tonight," Sensei broached the subject. "The truth is, I'm not myself either. I suppose you've noticed."

I had no answer to give.

"I quarreled with my wife earlier. I let petty emotions get the better of me."

"Why did you. . ." I couldn't bring myself to voice the word quarrel.

"My wife misunderstands me. And when I try to tell her so, she refuses to listen. I got cross with her."

"In what way does she misunderstand you?"

Sensei did not respond directly to my question. "If I were the kind of man she thinks I am, then I'd have no need to suffer so."

The nature and extent of Sensei's suffering were entirely unknown to me.

Chapter 10

On the way home, we walked in silence for several blocks. Then Sensei suddenly spoke. "I've done a bad thing. I left in anger, and my wife must be worried. A woman's lot, when I think of it, cannot be easy. My wife has no one in this world but me."

Sensei stopped speaking, but he seemed to expect no response. Shortly, he continued on. "Not to imply that a husband is entirely self-reliant. That would be a bit presumptuous. Tell me, how do I appear to you? Do you see me as self-possessed, or do I strike you as insecure?"

"Somewhere in between," I replied. This answer caught Sensei a little off guard. He said no more, and we walked on in silence.

The way back toward Sensei's house led us past my lodgings. We came to my corner, but I felt it improper to part from him there. "Let me accompany you on your way," I offered.

With an immediate wave of his hand, he declined. "It's already late, go on home. I need to get home too, for my wife's sake."

With those final words from Sensei, "for my wife's sake," a warm glow rose in my heart. Because of those words, I was able to return home and rest easy. For a long while thereafter, "for my wife's sake," remained in my mind.

The discord between Sensei and his wife, I knew, was of no real consequence. My continued visits to their home only served to confirm my supposition that such instances were, indeed, rare. In fact, Sensei once divulged to me the following.

"There's really only one woman in my world. Aside from my wife, the charms of no others entice me. My wife, for her part, treats me like I'm the only man in existence. We should be, by all accounts, the happiest of couples."

I've forgotten the circumstances that brought out this affirmation. I can't say clearly what transpired before or after. However, I do still remember that Sensei spoke in an earnest and somber tone. What struck me as odd at the time were Sensei's final words. "We should be, by all accounts, the happiest of couples." Why was Sensei unable to profess his happiness? Why did he qualify it with "should be?" This raised some doubt in my mind, especially with the emphasis he'd placed on these words. I wondered if Sensei was indeed happy, or if he meant that he should be happy but in fact was not. His words left me puzzled, but before long I had set the problem aside and moved on.

I called once in Sensei's absence and had occasion to talk with his wife. Sensei had left for Shinbashi to see off a friend who was sailing from Yokohama that day on a steamer bound for foreign lands. It was customary at the time for anyone sailing from Yokohama to take the eight thirty train from Shinbashi station. I was in need of Sensei's help with a certain passage, and I arrived at nine as we'd arranged. Sensei's outing to Shinbashi had been decided the day before on short notice as courtesy to his friend, who had called on him to bid farewell. Saying that he would return soon, Sensei had left instructions to have me wait in his absence. I was led to the parlor, and while I waited I conversed with Sensei's wife.

Chapter 11

By that time, I was a graduate student. Compared to the days of my early visits with Sensei, I felt myself much more an adult. I had come to know Sensei's wife quite well, and I was fully at ease in her presence. When I saw her, we talked on various subjects. However, our talk was always casual in nature, and I can't recall now what was said. Only one thing remains in my mind. Before relating it, though, there's another matter I should touch upon first.

Sensei was a university graduate. I knew this from the start. What I didn't know was that he had pursued no occupation. I learned this only after returning to Tōkyō. I wondered how he was able to do this, and why he should choose to.

Sensei was completely unknown to the world. I was, I expect, on account of the bond formed between us, the only one to appreciate his scholarship and hold his ideas in esteem. On numerous occasions I lamented this state of affairs. Sensei would merely dismiss my concerns with, "A man like myself has no business preaching to others." I found this reply excessively modest, so much so that it might, I thought, mask some form of contempt. In fact, Sensei would sometimes bring up a former classmate, who was now celebrated in his field, and level a scathing critique. I once took occasion to comment frankly on the contradiction I saw in this. I did it not to provoke him, but rather from frustration that the world should be indifferent toward him. Sensei replied in a subdued voice, "You must understand, there's nothing I can do. I'm a man unfit to answer society's call." There was a certain kind of profound look etched on his face. I didn't know if it was despondence, discontent, or sorrow, but its intensity overwhelmed me. I didn't have the courage to challenge him further.

As I talked with Sensei's wife, our discussion, in due course, fell first to Sensei and then to this very subject.

"How can Sensei be so studious in his own home yet not engaged with the world outside?"

"Engagement is out of the question. He won't even think of it."

"Because he views it as futile?"

"I can't say how he views the world—as a woman it's not my prerogative to know. However, I don't believe that's the case. I think he wants to engage. He wants to, but he can't. It's terribly unfortunate."

"But he seems quite capable. He's perfectly healthy, is he not?"

"His health is fine. There's nothing wrong with him."

"Then what could stop him from pursuing an occupation?"

"I'm afraid I can't tell you. If I knew that much, then I wouldn't worry so. I'm in the dark, unable to ease his plight."

In her voice was great sympathy. Still, she managed to put on a faint smile. On the surface at least, I was the more intent one, brooding in silence. As if suddenly remembering, she spoke again.

"He wasn't always like this. He was a different man in his youth. He's changed completely."

"How long ago do you mean?"

"His student days."

"You knew Sensei in his student days?"

She blushed a bit.

Chapter 12

Sensei's wife was a native of Tōkyō. I'd heard this through Sensei, and I'd also heard it directly from her. "I'm actually a child of mixed blood," she'd told me. She'd said this half-jokingly, as her father hailed from the Tottori region, and her mother was born in Ichigaya, back in the time when Tōkyō was still called Edo. Sensei, for his part, was a native of Niigata, an altogether different region. Any knowledge she had of Sensei's student days was clearly not through hometown connections. Having blushed a bit at my question, she seemed reluctant to expound further. I refrained from pressing the matter.

From the time I met Sensei until the time of his passing, I was exposed to his thoughts and sentiments through discourse on myriad topics. However, I learned very little of the circumstances surrounding his courtship and marriage. At times I credited him for his exercise of discretion. As an older man, he knew to spare a younger listener from amorous reminiscences. At other times, though, I faulted him for it. Sensei, and his wife too for that matter, had both come of age in an earlier time whose social conventions differed from those of today. Their generation, it seemed, was incapable of acknowledging romance. These were both, of course, nothing more than conjecture on my part. Behind both conjectures was my supposition of an impassioned courtship, one that still lent its warmth to the heart of their marriage.

My supposition, to be sure, was not in error. However, the romance I imagined in my head was only half the story. Beneath the beauty of their romance lurked a dreadful misfortune. Completely unbeknownst to his wife, this misfortune was tearing at Sensei's soul. To this day, she still doesn't know. Sensei carried his secret to the grave. Rather than destroy his wife's happiness, he chose to destroy himself.

I won't talk here of this misfortune. The affection between Sensei and his wife, which was in some sense inseparable from the misfortune that underpinned it, was indeed as just described. Neither talked much of their courtship. Sensei's wife for modesty's sake, and Sensei himself for deeper reasons.

There was, however, one incident that comes to mind. It was the season of blossoms, and Sensei and I were in Ueno. We saw a handsome couple, strolling closely arm in arm. The place being what it was, there were many sightseers, some of whom took more interest in this couple than the blossoms.

"A newly married couple," Sensei remarked.

"They seem quite taken with each other," I replied.

Sensei did not so much as feign a grin. He changed direction, removing the couple from our view. Then he asked me, "Have you ever been in love?"

I told him no.

"Do you ever wish you were?"

I didn't answer.

"I imagine you sometimes think of it."

"Yes."

"Your remark toward that couple was rather dismissive. I also sensed in it, though, the discontent of a man who thirsts for love but hasn't found it."

"Is that how it came across?"

"Yes. Any man knowing love would have spoken with greater warmth. However. . . , listen to me, love is iniquity. Mark my words."

This caught me off guard. I said nothing in response.

Chapter 13

We were amongst the crowds. All around us were happy faces. Until we'd moved on to the woods, away from both blossoms and people, there was no opportunity to continue on this topic.

"Love is iniquity?" I asked abruptly as we entered the woods.

"It is, without a doubt, iniquity." Sensei's reply was no less emphatic than before.

"How so?"

"You'll understand in time. Then again, you may understand already. Isn't there some aching in your heart, there for a good while now, that's stirred by love?"

I paused for a moment to reflect on my innermost feelings. Contrary to Sensei's premise, there was nothing there. Nothing at all came to mind.

"My heart, as clear as I can reckon, has nothing for which it aches. I wouldn't hesitate to confide in you if it did."

"That's precisely why it aches. It lacks any object of affection, and it won't find peace until it's grasped one."

"At present, I can't say it bothers me."

"You're somehow unfulfilled. Isn't that what brings you to seek my counsel?"

"That may be the case, but it's not related to love."

"It's a step on the path toward love. The bond you've formed with me is but preparation for the greater bond you'll form with a woman someday."

"The two things strike me as entirely dissimilar."

"No, they're the same. As a man, of course, I can never satisfy the aching in your heart. Furthermore, there are certain circumstances that render me of much less use to you than I should be. Of this I'm truly sorry, for your sake. You'll have to turn away from me and go elsewhere. I'm even compelled to hope that you do. However. . ."

I felt a strange sense of sorrow.

"If you're convinced that I'll turn away from you, then so be it, but the thought's never crossed my mind."

Sensei paid no heed to my words. "You have to be vigilant. Love is, indeed, iniquity. While you won't find contentment in my company, you won't face peril either.—Do you know how it feels to be bound by long black hair?"

I could imagine what he meant, but it was not something I'd ever experienced. At any rate, what Sensei meant by "love is iniquity" was not at all clear to me. I was growing a bit uncomfortable.

"Sensei, explain to me clearly how love is iniquity. Otherwise, let's leave this subject for another day, some day when I might understand."

"Forgive me. I'd intended to share a truth with you, but I've only confused the matter. I shouldn't have done that."

We strolled on at a leisurely pace, passing behind the museum and on toward Uguisudani. A thicket of bamboo grass, growing in seclusion in one corner of a vast garden, was visible through gaps in the fence.

"Do you know why I visit my friend's grave in Zōshigaya each month?"

Sensei's question was entirely out of the blue, and he knew very well that I had no answer. I refrained for a bit from replying. Sensei, realizing as much, spoke further. "Forgive me again. I felt bad for confusing you, and in thinking to explain things I've only made matters worse. It's no use. Let's leave it at that. Anyway, love is iniquity. Trust me. But it's also divine."

Sensei's words only confounded things further. However, he spoke no more on love.

Chapter 14

As a young man, I was prone to take counsel of my passions. That, at least, was how Sensei saw me. More than the lectures at school, I cherished my talks with him. More than the opinions of professors, I valued his insights. In short, more than the distinguished men who instructed me from their lecterns, I held in esteem the reticent and reclusive Sensei.

"You mustn't put me on a pedestal," Sensei once cautioned me.

"My opinion of you is rational and grounded," I answered back in full confidence.

Sensei did not share my conviction. "You've let yourself be carried away. When you see me for what I am, you'll come to despise me. As it is, I bear your respect as a burden. However, what troubles me most is the thought of how you'll change, of how you must change."

"Do you think me so fickle, so untrustworthy?"

"I can't help but pity you."

"You say you pity me, but you also imply you can't trust me."

Sensei turned toward the garden, a troubled look on his face. On the camellia bush, which had recently dazzled with brilliant splashes of red, not a single flower remained. Sensei was fond of gazing on this bush from his parlor.

"As far as trust is concerned, I don't distrust you in particular. It's all of humanity whom I distrust."

In that moment a voice, sounding like a goldfish vendor, sounded from beyond the hedge. Other than that, there was not a sound to be heard. The small lane, set back several blocks from the main thoroughfare, was surprisingly quiet. As always, all was still within the house. I knew that Sensei's wife was in the next room. I also knew she could hear my voice as she worked silently at her sewing or other tasks. At the same time, however, I was oblivious to her presence.

"Then you don't trust even your wife?" I asked.

Sensei looked a little uneasy. He did not answer me directly. "I don't trust even myself. If I can't trust myself, then how can I trust another? I'm cursed by my own soul."

"You're thinking too critically. Who could withstand such scrutiny?"

"No, it's not how I think, it's what I've done. I've been shocked, then later horrified, by my own actions."

I wanted to pursue this further, but Sensei's wife called out to him from the next room. He asked what it was, and she replied that she needed him for a moment. He went to her, and what transpired I cannot say. I had little time to wonder, as he quickly returned to the parlor.

"At any rate, you mustn't place your faith in me. You'll only regret it. You'll come to feel deluded and retaliate most callously."

"I'm not sure what you're implying."

"The thought that you once admired a man will drive you later to tear him down. To preclude your future disdain, I wish to forgo your present admiration. I prefer my current loneliness to a future that's lonelier still. For this modern age, with its personal freedoms, independent thought, and egotistical pursuits, loneliness is the price we pay."

Faced with such resignation from Sensei, I could offer no response.

Chapter 15

Thereafter, the sight of Sensei's wife evoked my concern. I wondered if Sensei's demeanor toward her was always such, and if so, did it not upset her.

From appearances, I couldn't judge if she were troubled or not. Part of the problem was that I didn't often see her. And when I did see her, I detected nothing unusual. Finally, we rarely interacted if not in Sensei's presence.

My misgivings didn't end there. I wondered about Sensei's resignation toward humanity. Was it simply the consequence of rational introspection? A product of detached observation of the modern age? Sensei was wont to sit and think. With a mind like his, did such resignation arise as a matter of course in reaction to the world? I couldn't accept that this was wholly the case. Sensei's resignation seemed to harbor a passion. It wasn't the cooled remains of some burned-out stone structure. Sensei, in my eyes, was a thinking man. However, behind the doctrine this thinking man had arrived at, some powerful truth seemed to resonate. It didn't belong to the people he'd pushed away. It was a truth felt keenly and first hand, a truth that had made his blood race, a truth that had made his heart skip. Such a truth, it seemed, was layered throughout his thoughts.

This was more than gut instinct on my part. Sensei himself had confessed as much. His confession, though, was like a rampart in the sky. It hung above my head, and it frightened me, though I couldn't quite say why. Sensei's confession was murky at best. Perhaps for this reason it unsettled me so.

I supposed that Sensei's worldview had been shaped by passionate love (occurring, of course, between Sensei and his wife). Sensei's insistence that love is iniquity was partly what led me to this supposition. However, Sensei had told me himself how deeply he cared for his wife. How could their love, then, have led him to despondent resignation? Sensei had told me, "The thought that you once admired a man will drive you later to tear him down." These words were directed, it seemed, to the modern world in a general way. They did not apply to Sensei and his wife.

The grave in Zōshigaya, whomever it might belong to, crossed my mind from time to time. I knew that Sensei felt a deep connection to it. It occupied a corner in his mind, and as I strived to be close to him, I couldn't help but focus my thoughts on it. To me, though, it was something utterly lifeless. It would never serve to draw us together. In fact, it stood between us, like an apparition, inhibiting our intimacy.

By and by, another occasion brought me face to face with Sensei's wife. It was late autumn, with a marked chill already in the air, and folks hurrying on their ways through waning daylight. Over a short period, a number of homes in Sensei's neighborhood had been burglarized, all in the evening hours. In most cases, nothing of great value was taken. Nevertheless, in all cases, something or other was missing. Sensei's wife was on edge, and on one particular evening Sensei could not stay home with her. A friend from his home town, now serving at a provincial hospital, had come to Tōkyō. Sensei, along with several other gentlemen, had arranged to take this friend to dinner. Sensei explained the circumstances to me and asked if I could mind the house in his absence. I readily accepted.

Chapter 16

I arrived in the early evening, just as lights were coming on in the houses. Sensei, who was by nature a punctual man, was already gone.

"He left just a moment ago," Sensei's wife explained. "He didn't want to risk being late." She guided me to Sensei's study.

Aside from a desk and chair, there were numerous books arranged in cabinets. Their handsome bindings were illuminated by the electric light that shone through the glass. Sensei's wife directed me to a seating cushion that she'd set out before the brazier. She told me to help myself to Sensei's books, and then she took her leave. I felt a bit awkward, like a guest waiting for the master of the house to return. I remained where I was, rooted to my cushion, and had a smoke. I could hear voices from the hearth room. Sensei's wife was explaining something to the maidservant. To get to the study, one could follow the hearth room veranda to its end and turn the corner. From a floor plan perspective, it was off in its own corner, quieter yet than the parlor. After a while, the conversation in the hearth room ceased, and the house fell silent. I imagined myself lying in wait for a burglar. I kept still and maintained my vigilance.

Thirty minutes passed. Sensei's wife reappeared at the study entrance and looked at me with mild surprise.

I was still formally seated, like a guest in waiting.

"You should make yourself comfortable."

"I'm comfortable like this."

"You're not bored?"

"Not at all. Not with the thought of a burglar about."

She stood there smiling, a tea cup in her hand.

"Perhaps," I added, "this corner of the house is not so ideal for keeping watch."

"Might I suggest that you relocate closer to the center? I thought you might be bored here and made you a cup of tea. If you don't mind moving, I'll serve you in the hearth room."

I left the study and followed Sensei's wife to the hearth room, where an iron kettle whistled on a handsome brazier. I was served tea there and treated to sweets. Sensei's wife did not take any tea. She said it would keep her from sleeping.

"Does Sensei sometimes participate in such gatherings then?"

"Very rarely. Lately he seems less and less fond of company."

Sensei's wife, as she said this, gave no indication of being particularly troubled by it. Feeling emboldened, I pursued the subject further. "Then you're his one exception, I suppose."

"No, I'm no different from the rest."

"That can't be the case," I replied. "And I expect you know it's not the case."

"Why is that?"

"Because, as I see it, it's his fondness for you that lets him forget the world."

"Like all good scholars, you're practiced in eloquence, but your logic rings hollow. Couldn't you as well have argued that in spurning the world he has to spurn me as well? The logic is equally sound."

"I could have argued either way, but the argument I chose, in this case, is the correct one."

"I've no wish to debate you. Men love to argue for argument's sake. It never ceases to amaze me, how they amuse themselves exchanging empty cups."

Her words were somewhat harsh, but they weren't delivered with full force. Sensei's wife was not so modern as to wield her intellect for personal conquest. She seemed intent, rather, on dispensing with the superficial in favor of deeper truths.

Chapter 17

There was more that I wanted to say. However, I did not wish her to see me as the argumentative male, so I held my tongue. As I gazed into the bottom of my empty tea cup, she re-engaged me by offering to refill it. I handed her the cup.

"How many? One? Two?"

She held a cube of sugar with a curious utensil. She was looking at me to ask how many I'd like in my tea. Her manner seemed somewhat contrite. She was trying, through use of feminine charm, to soften the blow of her earlier words.

I drank my tea in silence. The cup was empty, and still I held my silence.

"You've become awfully quiet," she remarked.

"I'm afraid," I answered, "that should I speak, you'll dismiss me as argumentative."

"I promise not to," she assured me.

We began conversing again, and the subject of our conversation soon returned to Sensei, in whom we shared a common interest.

"Can I continue a bit where we left off previously. It may have struck you as empty argument, but to me it was no such thing."

"Alright then."

"Suppose that Sensei suddenly lost you. Do you think he could carry on?"

"Now how would I know? If you want an answer to that, you'd best ask Sensei. It's really not for me to say."

"But I'm serious. You mustn't evade the question. Tell me honestly what you think."

"I've told you already. I honestly wouldn't know."

"Tell me this then. How much do you love Sensei? This is something that you can answer better than Sensei, so I'm asking you."

"There's no need to ask so directly, is there?"

"You mean there's no need to seriously pose this question, because the answer is already self-evident?"

"Yes, I suppose so."

"Sensei has in you, then, a devoted companion. If he suddenly lost you, how do you think he would fare? How would this man, who takes no interest in the outside world, cope without you? I'm not asking how

Sensei would see this, I'm asking how you see it. In your opinion, would Sensei be happy or unhappy?"

"I can tell you how I see it. (Sensei may or may not agree.) Sensei would be most unhappy without me. He might even lose his will to carry on. This may sound pretentious, but I believe I make Sensei as happy as is humanly possible. I'm convinced that no one else could make him as happy as I do. That's why we live so peaceably together."

"Sensei, I believe, cannot help but sense and cherish your conviction."

"That's another matter."

"You still fear that he doesn't find favor with you?"

"It's not so much that he doesn't find favor with me. There's no reason he shouldn't. However, he's turned his back on the world. Or rather, of late, he's lost all faith in humanity. If he's lost all faith in humanity, then how can he embrace me, his fellow human?"

I understood her meaning now. How she saw herself as cut loose by Sensei, the two of them drifting apart.

Chapter 18

Sensei's wife impressed me with her insight. Her thought process differed from that of a traditional Japanese woman, and this too greatly piqued my interest. Furthermore, she spoke plainly, eschewing the use of "modern" words that had, of late, come into common use.

I myself was an imprudent young man, yet to experience any meaningful female contact. As a man, of course, I was drawn to the opposite sex, and in my musings, women were a constant object of desire. In my musings, though, I evoked these women only vaguely. I saw them as lovely clouds, floating by on enchanting springtime breezes. When confronted with a real woman, my feelings were prone to tumultuous change. Rather than feel attraction, I might well be gripped by an odd sense of repulsion. Sensei's wife, though, had no such effect on me. That gulf between men and women, who view the world so differently, was hardly apparent. I was no longer conscious of conversing with a woman. She was simply another who, through faithful observation and sympathetic reflection, knew Sensei well.

"A while back, when I asked you why Sensei had disengaged from the world, there was something you said to me. You told me he'd changed."

"He really has changed. He wasn't like this before."

"What was he like."

"He was exactly what we both wish him to be—a man full of promise."

"How could he have changed so abruptly?"

"It wasn't abrupt. It happened gradually, over time."

"And you were by him all this time?"

"Of course. We're husband and wife."

"Then you must, I expect, have some idea what caused him to change."

"That's what troubles me. I wish I had an answer, but I honestly just don't know. I've begged him so often to open himself to me, to share what he's feeling."

"What does he say?"

"He says it's just his nature. There's nothing to be said, and there's no need to worry. He won't confide in me."

I listened in silence. She stopped there. The maidservant, in her quarters, made not a sound. I'd forgotten the burglar completely.

"You don't think I'm to blame, do you?" she suddenly asked me.

"No," I answered.

"Tell me the truth. I couldn't bear for you to think of me thus." She continued. "I like to believe that I'm doing all I can on Sensei's behalf."

"Rest assured, you are. I can attest that Sensei knows it."

She leveled the coals in the brazier and replenished the iron kettle. The kettle's singing was quickly quenched.

"I finally came to my wit's end and confronted him. I implored him to tell me my faults. I promised I'd try to do better. He told me it wasn't me, that the fault lay with him. I became despondent and burst into tears. More than ever, I wished for his rebuke."

Her eyes were moist with tears.

Chapter 19

Initially, I'd engaged with Sensei's wife as a partner in rational discourse. As we'd spoken, though, her manner had gradually changed. Instead of appealing to my reason, she began to touch my emotions. There was no ill will between her and Sensei, nor should there have been. Yet something was wrong. Then again, on closer inspection, there was nothing to be found. Such was the nature of her angst.

She had first asserted that since Sensei was weary of the world he must also be weary of her. Even while asserting this, she was not fully satisfied with it. Digging deeper, the converse had also crossed her mind. She imagined that Sensei's displeasure with her had turned him away from the world in general. However, try as she might, she could not substantiate this fear. Sensei's demeanor was that of the good husband. He was always kind and caring. Day by day, though, she'd harbored shades of doubt and tucked them away in the depths of her bosom. On this evening, she brought them forth in my presence.

"What do you think," she asked, "is it my doing? Or is it as you said, that his view of the world has somehow disturbed him? Please be candid."

I had no intention of being anything but candid. However, if there were facts unknown to me, and I believed that indeed there were, then any answer I gave would certainly prove inadequate.

"I don't know."

Her look at that moment was one of dismay, of one who's hopes had been dashed. I immediately added to my answer. "But I can assure you that Sensei holds you in highest regard. I've heard this from him directly, and Sensei is nothing if not an honest man."

She gave no reply. After a while she spoke further. "There is one thing that comes to mind. . ."

"You mean to explain Sensei's temperament?"

"Yes. And if it were to be the cause, then I wouldn't have to worry it might be me. That alone would be a great relief."

"What is it you're thinking?"

She gazed at her hands, which were resting on her thighs, seemingly reluctant to continue. "Here it is then. Give me your opinion."

"I'll do my best."

"I can't tell you everything. Sensei would be terribly upset if I did. I'll tell you just what I can."

I swallowed tensely.

"In his student days at the university, Sensei had one very close friend. Shortly before graduation, that friend died. He died unexpectedly." She leaned close to my ear and added in a whisper, "He died an unnatural death."

When she told me this, I couldn't help but ask how he'd died.

"That's all I'm at liberty to say. But it was after his death that Sensei began to change. I don't know what led to his death, and I suspect that Sensei may not know either. However, it's not inconceivable that his death is tied to Sensei's change."

"Is the grave in Zōshigaya that of this friend?"

"I've promised never to speak of that, so I won't. Could the death of one close friend affect a person so? That's what I need to know. I'd like your opinion on this."

It seemed, in my mind, not likely.

Chapter 20

Based on what little I knew, I did my best to console her. Sensei's wife, for her part, tried to find comfort in my company. We continued conversing on this same subject. However, I was far from grasping the heart of the matter. Her disquiet stemmed from misgivings, and those misgivings, in turn, were but as an errant wisp of telltale vapor. When it came to the true nature of things, there was much that she herself didn't know. What she did know, she was not at liberty to disclose in full. Thus it was that I, who sought to console her, and she, who sought comfort, were like two souls adrift on the waves. To steady herself, she reached out her hand to me, latching on to my equally ungrounded counsel.

Around ten o'clock, the sound of Sensei's footsteps echoed in the entryway. His wife, seeming to brush aside all that we'd been speaking of, immediately sprang to her feet. Leaving me behind, she rushed out to greet Sensei, almost bumping into him as he slid open the panel. I followed after as fast as I could. Only the maidservant, who must have been dozing, failed to appear.

Sensei was in good spirits. His wife, however, looked happier still. I recalled how moments earlier her brow had been drawn tight and her delicate eyes had glistened with tears. The transformation was extraordinary. Assuming it was not all a ruse (and I couldn't imagine that it was), then it was entirely possible that I'd been played upon, in some mischievous female fashion, for the sake of my sentiment. In that moment, though, I wasn't wont to view Sensei's wife in such light. The lifting of her spirits, rather, relieved me. I realized then that I needn't have been so concerned.

"Thank you for securing the fort," Sensei said to me with a grin. "I take it the burglar didn't show? I hope you weren't disappointed."

As I prepared to depart, Sensei's wife thanked me for my trouble. More than the trouble of an evening away from my studies, she seemed to refer, half-jokingly, to the trouble of staking out a burglar in vain. As she spoke, she pressed a paper-wrapped package into my hands. It was the remainder of the sweets she'd served me earlier. I dropped it into my sleeve pocket and stepped out into the evening chill. Winding my way through the empty side streets, I hurried on toward the lights of the town.

I've related in detail all that I remember of that evening. I've related it because it bears relating. The truth, however, is that the conversation of that night, as I made my way home with my package of sweets, did not strike me as all that important. The following day, I came home from school for lunch and found the package of sweets on my desk, where I'd set it the night before. I immediately unwrapped it, picked out a reddish brown piece of castella spread with chocolate, and bit off a large piece. As I savored the cake, I thought of the couple from whom I'd received it, a happy pair together against the world.

Autumn gave way uneventfully to winter. I continued my visits to Sensei's home. When I was there, I sometimes asked his wife for help in washing and mending my clothes. I'd never worn undergarments, but I began at this time to sport a black collared garment over my undershirt. Sensei's wife, who had no children to mind, was happy to assist me. It kept her busy, she said, and the physical work did her good.

"This is hand woven. I've never sewn such fine fabric. It's not easy, though, to put a needle through it. I've broken two already."

Even when she voiced such objections, her expression assured me that she was not in the least put out.

Chapter 21

That winter, I was unexpectedly called home. I received a letter from my mother informing me that my father's illness had taken a turn for the worse. There was no immediate concern, but he was on in years, so I should make my way home as soon as possible.

My father's kidneys had been troubling him for some time. As often happens past middle age, his malady had turned chronic. At the same time, both my father and the family were confident that with proper care his condition was more or less manageable. To visitors, he would even declare that he owed his survival to prudent rest and judicious recovery. Then one day, according to my mother's letter, after an outing in the garden he'd grown dizzy and fallen. Members of the household, assuming he'd suffered a mild stroke, immediately treated him accordingly. The doctor, however, on examining him later, was of a different opinion, linking the incident to the state of his kidneys. The family had not theretofore associated kidney disease with swooning.

It was only a short while till winter break, and I saw no problem in waiting for the term to end. However, from time to time over the next several days I imagined my father in bed and the worried look on my mother's face. These visions nipped at my conscience, until finally I resolved to return. To save the time and trouble of remittance, I decided to ask Sensei to advance me travel money when I called to take my leave.

Sensei, who was down with a touch of a cold, had me shown directly to his study. Warm sunlight, so rarely seen since the onset of winter, shone through the glass doors and fell across the surface of his desk. In the middle of this well-lit room, Sensei had placed a large brazier. To help him breathe easier, a metal basin had been filled with water and placed on the kettle stand. Steam wafted up from the basin.

"I'd rather it were something serious. These minor colds are the worst thing of all." Sensei looked at me with a wry smile as he spoke.

This from a man who'd never in his life been seriously ill. I couldn't help but smile.

"I'd gladly take a cold in exchange for something worse. I expect you would too, if you once fell truly ill."

"I don't know. If I ever do fall ill, then I'd just as well fall deathly ill."

I dismissed this as idle chatter, proceeded to relate the contents of my mother's letter, and asked if I might borrow some money.

"I'm sorry to hear about your father. We should have adequate cash on hand."

Sensei summoned his wife and had her bring the required amount. She carefully laid out the money, which she'd gone in and pulled from a drawer in the cupboard or elsewhere, on a sheet of white paper that she'd set out before me. "You must be concerned."

"Are his fainting spells frequent?" Sensei asked.

"There was nothing about that in the letter—is it something that recurs?"

"Yes."

I learned for the first time that Sensei's wife's mother had died of the same illness.

"That doesn't sound good," I said.

"I'm afraid not. I'd take his place for you if I could—has he felt nauseous?"

"I don't know. There was no mention of it, so I expect not."

"If he's not nauseous then he's still all right," Sensei's wife added.

I left Tōkyō that same day on the evening train.

Chapter 22

Father's condition was not as bad as I'd feared. Even so, when I arrived I found him sitting in bed.

"Everyone's worried, so I'm biding my time. I'm well enough to get up," he told me.

The very next day, despite my mother's objections, he did get out of bed. "Now that you're home, your father suddenly has his energy back," my mother remarked as she reluctantly folded away the thick futon. It seemed to me, though, that he was not just putting on a brave face—he really did look okay.

My older brother had taken on work in far off Kyūshū. Under all but the most pressing circumstances, it was not easy for him to make his way back. My younger sister had married a man in another province, and she too was not easily summoned home. Of us three siblings, it was me, the student, who was most at the ready to come when called. Father took great satisfaction in the fact that I'd put aside my studies for his sake and come home early at mother's behest.

"I'm sorry we've disrupted your studies. It was really nothing serious. Mother overstates things in her letters." Father spoke thus, and once he was out of bed, he did indeed seem back to his usual self.

"Don't overdo it, or you'll end up back in bed."

Father appreciated my concern but paid little heed to my warning. "I'm fine. I know my limitations."

He did, in fact, look fine. As he moved about the house, there was no shortness of breath, and he experienced no dizzy spells. His complexion was terribly pale, but this had been the case for quite some while, so we saw no particular cause for concern.

I wrote to Sensei to thank him for the loan. I told him I would repay him in person after my return to Tōkyō in the new year, and I asked for his patience until that time. I followed with news from home—father's condition was not as serious as I'd feared; at this rate we could rest assured for a while; there were no further spells of vertigo and no signs of nausea. In closing, I added my wishes for Sensei's recovery from his cold, which I knew to be nothing severe.

I posted my letter, with no expectation of receiving a reply. After I sent it, I talked with my mother and father of Sensei. As we talked, I pictured in my mind his distant study.

"When you return to Tōkyō, you should take him some mushrooms."

"I could, but I wonder if he eats dried mushrooms."

"They're nothing special, but I've never known anyone to dislike them."

Somehow Sensei and dried mushrooms struck me as incongruous.

I was caught by surprise when a letter arrived from Sensei. I was especially surprised to find that it contained nothing of particular importance. Sensei had written me solely out of kindness. Looking at it in this light, this single short letter warmed my heart, even more so since it was the first letter Sensei wrote me.

In stating that this was my first letter from Sensei, I don't mean to imply that we ever became frequent correspondents. Quite to the contrary, in fact, I received only two letters from Sensei during his lifetime.

The first was this brief reply that I've just mentioned. The second was a lengthy piece that he wrote to me shortly before his death.

My father, due to the nature of his illness, was limited in his activities. Even after getting out of bed, he seldom ventured outdoors. On one afternoon, when the weather was unseasonably mild, he did go down to the garden. I stayed at his side the entire time, on the off chance that something should happen. I asked him to keep his hand on my shoulder, but he countered with a grin that he could manage just fine.

Chapter 23

I kept my father company and helped him pass the time, often in front of the shōgi board. Indulging our indolence, we sunk ourselves into the kotatsu, the game board placed over its frame. After each move, we'd retract our hands to the warmth of the quilting. From time to time we'd lose a captured piece, only discovering its absence when we went to start our next game. I can picture still my mother discovering a piece among the ashes and retrieving it with the fire tongs.

"The go board is too thick, especially with its feet, for play on the kotatsu. This shōgi board is just right. We can play in comfort. Perfect for a couple of idlers. How 'bout another game?"

Father would always call for another game after winning. He would call for one after losing too. In short, whether he won or he lost, he was content to settle into the kotatsu and play shōgi. This retirement-like lifestyle was something novel to me, and for a while I embraced its amusements. As the days and hours passed, though, the energy of youth made me restless for something more. I'd stretch my arms above my head, gripping a shōgi piece, a gold general or a lance, in my fist. Sometimes I'd even yawn overtly.

I thought about Tōkyō. I listened to the rhythm of my heart as my blood swelled and raced within it.

Strangely, in the right state of consciousness, I could feel Sensei lending vigor to the pulse of that rhythm.

Inwardly, I compared my father and Sensei. Both lived quiet lives, the outside world oblivious to their existence. In terms of societal impact, both men registered nil. Be that as it may, I found this father of mine, who sought to engage me in shōgi for the sake of diversion, somehow lacking. Sensei, with whom I'd never shared such pastimes, touched my mind more profoundly than any companion in amusements ever could have. To say he touched my mind is too cerebral. I should rather say he moved my heart. To state that his spirit energized my flesh, or that his life force coursed through my veins, by no means exaggerates my feelings of that time. When I looked about me, the obvious yet inconvenient fact that I was my father's son, while Sensei was a complete stranger, left me unsettled.

About the time I began feeling restless, the novelty of my presence was also wearing off for my mother and father. Little by little, they tired of me. Anyone, I expect, who's returned to the country for summer vacation or some such occasion has experienced like feelings. After being fussed over excessively for the first week or so, there comes a point where the magic is exhausted, and hospitality drops to the level of indifference or disregard. In the course of my stay, I passed this point. To make matters worse, I always came home with a piece of Tōkyō in me, something alien to my mother and father. In former times, this might be akin to stepping into a Confucian household steeped in Christian beliefs. My mother and father were not at all amenable to the changes they saw. I had no intention of offending their sensibilities, but I couldn't conceal who I was. Despite my best efforts, things would catch their attention. Life at home was an ever-increasing strain. I couldn't wait to return to Tōkyō.

Fortunately, my father's condition seemed stable. There were no indications he was failing. To be sure, we summoned a specialist from afar and had him conduct a thorough examination. He told us nothing we didn't already know. I decided to leave a little before the end of break. Once I announced my plans, my mother and father, true to human nature, entreated me to stay.

"Already? Do you have to go so soon?" my mother asked.

"You can stay a bit longer yet, can't you?" my father added.

I held firm and departed as planned.

Chapter 24

Back in Tōkyō, the festive pine ornaments had all been cleared away. A cold wind scoured the streets. Signs of the New Year were few and far between.

Without delay, I called on Sensei to return the money I'd borrowed. I also took with me the dried mushrooms from home. Uncomfortable simply handing them to Sensei's wife, I explained first that my mother had prepared them for me to bring as a gift. They were packed in a new cake box. Sensei's wife received them with due ceremony. She picked up the box to take it into the next room and, perhaps surprised at its lightness, asked what sort of cakes they were. Sensei's wife, once one came to know her, would sometimes display this overtly candid and child-like spirit.

The two of them, concerned for my father's health, asked various questions about his illness. Finally Sensei said, "From what you've told us, it seems he's not in immediate danger. Be careful, though. You mustn't drop your guard."

Sensei knew much more about kidney conditions than I did.

"The thing about kidney disease is that the afflicted party can often be blissfully ignorant. I know of a military officer who succumbed to it. His death was completely unexpected. His wife, who was sleeping at his side, didn't even have the chance to tend to him. He woke her once in the night, saying he felt a bit out of sorts, and the next morning he was gone. According to his wife, she'd thought he was still sleeping."

The optimism I'd been feeling quickly faded.

"I wonder about my father then. Could he meet the same end?"

"What did the doctor say?"

"That there's no way to cure him, but that he's all right for now."

"If that's what the doctor says, then I'm sure he's fine. The fellow I spoke of was unaware of his own condition. On top of that, he was a military man who didn't know his limitations."

I felt a bit better. Sensei, who'd been observing my mood, then added, "Human beings, whether healthy or sick, are truly fragile things. There's no telling who will go when, or in what manner."

"Then you think about such things too?"

"I may be in good health, but I can't say the thought never crosses my mind." Sensei showed a trace of a smile. "Some just slip away easily, in a natural manner. Others are taken in an instant, often through unnatural violence."

"What sort of unnatural violence?"

"I can't give specifics, but suicide would be an example. It's unnatural, and inevitably involves some form of violence."

"Those who are murdered, then, also die of unnatural violence."

"I hadn't thought of murder, but yes, that's the same kind of thing."

After that I returned home. Once home, I no longer dwelled on thoughts of my father. Nor did I fixate on Sensei's words. What he'd said about natural and unnatural death had been interesting in the moment, but I soon put it out of my mind. My graduation thesis, which I'd dabbled at in fits and starts, was looming before me. It was time to start writing in earnest.

Chapter 25

To graduate as intended in June, I was required to finish my thesis by the end of April. February, March, April—I counted off the remaining months on my fingers. I wondered if I could really pull it off. Most other students had started some time ago, busily gathering materials and preparing notes, while I had done almost nothing. All I had to my credit was my resolve to start in earnest in the new year. I acted on my resolve and rushed in, only to reach an immediate standstill. I'd been painting grand plans in my mind, framing a structure around my topic, and now I sat with head in hands, anxiety taking root. I narrowed the focus of my thesis. To save the exertion of refining and consolidating ideas, I decided to simply survey the literature and add to it an appropriate conclusion.

My chosen topic was closely connected to Sensei's area of expertise. Earlier, in making my choice, I'd solicited his opinion and received a favorable response. Still in a state of distress, I set out for Sensei's for guidance on essential references. Sensei was glad to share what he knew, and he even offered to lend me several books. However, he made it clear that he could not serve as an advisor.

"I don't read much these days, so I don't know what's new. It's best you consult with one of your professors."

I remembered learning from Sensei's wife that he'd once been an avid reader, but recently, for whatever reason, he'd lost interest. Forgetting my thesis for the moment, I inquired on this matter.

"Why don't you read like you used to?"

"There's no deep reason. . . maybe, at some point, I just decided it was all in vain. On top of that. . ."

"There's more to it yet?"

"Again, it's nothing profound. In my younger days, it was always awkward to be asked something and not have an answer—almost shameful. Lately, though, I've lost that feeling, and with it my drive to read up and stay current. In short, I'm old and decrepit."

Sensei spoke calmly. From this man who had turned his back on the world came no hint of bitterness. My reaction was accordingly muted. While I didn't view Sensei as old and decrepit, neither could I applaud his deportment. I took my leave.

From that day forward I toiled at my thesis like a man possessed, looking out on the world through bloodshot eyes. I approached my friends who'd graduated the year before to seek their advice. One of them told me how he'd rushed to the office in a rickshaw just prior to his deadline. Another told me how he'd nearly been rejected for delivering his thesis at fifteen minutes past five. Only by good graces of the department head was it accepted. I was still anxious, but I also felt emboldened. Day after day, I slaved away at my desk, testing my physical limits. If not at my desk, I was in the library, searching among the dimly-lit stacks. I scanned the gold-lettered bindings like a curio hunter let loose among ancient wares.

Plum blossoms appeared, and the cold north wind gradually shifted to a southern breeze. A short while later, talk of cherry blossoms caught my ear. Even so, I kept my eyes trained straight ahead like a cart horse, my thesis deadline forcing me on. Only after those final days of April, when I'd wrapped up my writing according to plan, did I again cross Sensei's threshold.

Chapter 26

I gained my freedom in early summer, just as the double-flowered cherry tree was shedding its last blossoms and starting to show the first faint signs of new green leaves. Like a songbird flown from its cage, I surveyed the world around me and reveled in my new-found freedom. I went at once to see Sensei. Along the way, my eyes were drawn to new buds bursting from the dark branches of a hedge. I also noticed shiny dull-brown leaves budding from a weathered pomegranate trunk, softly reflecting the warm sunlight. Never before had such things enchanted me so.

Sensei saw the joy in my face. "You finished your thesis, I take it. Well done."

"I did, thanks to your assistance. Everything's done."

I had, in fact, dispensed with all of my responsibilities. I felt relieved. From this point forward, I was free to flaunt my leisure. I was confident in the thesis I'd written, and satisfied with my effort. I couldn't refrain from explaining the work at length. Sensei humored me but offered no comment or critique beyond his usual subdued responses. I didn't feel dissatisfied, but I did feel a bit deflated. Even so, I was too full of life on this day to let his detachment go unchallenged. I decided to invite him outside, to witness the great rebirth—all of nature adorning itself in green.

"Sensei, let's go for a walk. It's wonderful out."

"Where to?"

It didn't matter to me where we went. I simply wished to stroll through nature with Sensei.

An hour later, we'd left the city behind us and were wandering through a quiet rural district. I plucked some tender new leaves off a hedge and made a grass whistle. I'd learned to whistle this way by watching a friend from Kagoshima, and I'd become quite good at it. I whistled on with great satisfaction, while Sensei looked about him, unimpressed with my talent.

By and by we came to a grove of trees, of medium height and thickly veiled in new leaves, through which a small lane passed. "Such-and-such Garden" was posted on the gatepost, so it was clearly not a private estate. Sensei looked at the gently ascending lane and suggested we take it. I replied that it looked to be a nursery.

We proceeded into the thicket, topped a low rise, and saw a house on the left. The shōji were open wide, but there were no inhabitants visible within. The only sign of life was a large bowl, set under the eaves, in which goldfish swam.

"It's quiet back here. Do you think it's okay to proceed unannounced?"

"I don't expect they'll mind."

We proceeded further, but saw not a soul. Azaleas bloomed in profusion, setting the scene ablaze with color. Sensei pointed out a taller bush of reddish yellow. "That must be kirishima."

A field was planted with peonies, but it was too early in the season for their flowers. At the edge of the peony field was a raised platform of weathered wood. Sensei laid himself out for a rest. I seated myself on the other edge for a smoke. Sensei gazed into the depths of the clear sky. I took in the colors of the new foliage around us. On close observation, all of the colors were subtly dissimilar. Even among the same variety of maple, no two trees were matched in hue. Sensei's hat, which he'd tossed over the top of a thin cedar sapling, was rocked by the breeze and dropped to the ground.

Chapter 27

I immediately picked up the hat. I used the backs of my nails to flick off specks of red clay and then called to Sensei.

"Your hat fell."

"Ah, thank you."

Sensei propped himself up and took the hat. Holding that same position, neither upright nor prone, he posed a curious question.

"If I may ask, is your family well off?"

"I wouldn't really say so."

"How much would you say you have? Forgive me for being so blunt."

"We own some property, fields and surrounding hills. Other than that, no savings to speak of."

This was the first time Sensei had ever asked directly about my family's finances. For my part, I'd never asked Sensei about his own circumstances. I had wondered, from the early days of our acquaintance, how he afforded his life of leisure. That question had remained with me, as I had never dared ask him point blank. Now, as I paused in my study of leaves and permitted my eyes a rest, the question was suddenly ripe for the asking.

"How about yourself? How wealthy are you?"

"Do I look like a man of means?"

Sensei was always modest in his dress. His household help was also limited. His house, in turn, was not a large one. It was clear, though, even to myself as an outsider, that he didn't want for material comforts. In short, while not extravagant, he wasn't scrimping and saving to get by.

"To some extent," I answered.

"I do have enough to maintain my current lifestyle, but by no means am I a wealthy man. If I were, I'd build a bigger place."

Sensei had raised himself and was now sitting cross-legged on the platform. As he finished speaking, he began to trace a circle on the ground with the tip of his bamboo walking stick. After closing the circle, he thrust his stick straight into the earth.

"I was in fact a wealthy man."

He seemed to be saying this more to himself than to me. The chance to respond in the moment evaded me, so I remained silent.

"You should know that I was once wealthy."

Sensei restated his thought, and this time looked my way with a smile. Even so, I still gave no reply. Or I should say, rather, that I was too unsettled to craft a response. In the meantime, Sensei shifted the conversation elsewhere.

"How is your father doing?"

Since New Year's, I'd had no further word on my father's health. The brief notes that accompanied my monthly remittance were in my father's hand as always, but he rarely made mention of his illness. His writing, though, was steady and sure. There was no sign whatsoever of trembling in the hands, as is common with his type of illness.

"I've heard nothing further, so I assume he's doing all right."

"I hope that's the case, but an illness like his is not to be taken lightly."

"Do you think his time may be near? He seems to be holding on. And he doesn't mention it in his notes."

"I see."

I took Sensei's questions on my family's assets and my father's health as normal conversation—as a natural voicing of the thoughts that came to his mind. To Sensei, however, these two topics were tightly intertwined, and the connection between them was highly significant. Not having the benefit of his experience, though, I did not know this at the time.

Chapter 28

I realize it's not my business, but if your family has wealth then I suggest you settle things soon. Best to receive your due while your father is still of sound mind. When something unforeseen happens, division of assets often sows discord."

"I see."

I didn't give much mind to Sensei's words. I wasn't worried for myself, nor for my father or mother. No one in my family, I believed, warranted such concern. Further, it was unlike Sensei to expound on a practical matter, and it caught me off guard. Deference to Sensei as my elder, however, compelled me to listen without reproach.

"Forgive me if talk of your father's death is uncomfortable, but all men must eventually die. Even a man in the best of health may go at any time."

Sensei's tone was unusually somber.

"Such talk doesn't bother me in the least." I cleared the way for Sensei to continue. "How many brothers and sisters did you say you have?" Sensei asked.

Sensei asked, in turn, about all the members of my immediate family. He also asked about my aunts and uncles and their circumstances. Finally he asked, "Are they all good people?"

"None strike me as dishonest. They're country folk, for the most part."

"What makes you so sure that country folk are honest?"

I struggled with this question. Sensei, for his part, did not wait on my answer.

"Country folk, it often turns out, are no less dishonest than city folk. Also, you told me just now that none among your relatives struck you as dishonest. Do you imagine, then, that humans are of two distinct types, upright and dishonest? There's no common mold from which scoundrels are cast. All men are virtuous most of the time. Or if they're not virtuous, they're at least ordinary. Then the moment of truth arrives, and the villain appears out of nowhere. It's a frightening world—you have to watch yourself."

Sensei was not finished, and I too had thoughts to share in response. We were interrupted, however, by the sudden barking of a dog behind us. We both turned round in surprise.

Cedar saplings had been planted near the rear of the platform, and next to them was a plot in which thick bamboo grass covered the ground. Only the head and back of the barking dog were visible within this grass.

A boy of about ten ran up and scolded the dog severely. Then he turned and greeted Sensei, his black insignia cap still on his head.

"Tell me sir, when you came in was there no one in the house?" he asked.

"No one was there."

"But they were. Mother and sister were in the kitchen."

"Were they?"

"You should have called hello on your way by."

Sensei managed a smile. He took his coin purse from his pocket and placed a five-sen piece in the boy's hand. "Give them my best regards, and allow us to rest here a while."

A smile beamed in the boy's sharp eyes as he nodded his agreement. "I'm the scout today."

With that, he ran downhill past the azaleas. The dog ran after, its tail raised high in the air. A short while later, several more boys of the same age appeared. They too then followed down the hill on the same trail as the scout.

Chapter 29

Due to the dog and the children, Sensei had not concluded his thoughts, and I was left hanging. Assets and the like, over which Sensei seemed so concerned, were of little interest to me at that time. Because of my nature, and perhaps too because of my circumstances, the concept of vying for gain was far from my mind. I was not on my own yet and had not been exposed to such matters. At any rate, my youthful self was utterly oblivious to issues of wealth.

There was one thing, though, on which I wanted to question Sensei further. He had said that when the moment of truth arrives, any man may emerge as a villain. I wanted to know what he meant. On the surface, or course, I understood his words well enough. There was certainly more to it, though, and I wanted to know the rest.

After the dog and the children had gone their way, the orchard fell back into silence. We sat motionless for a while, two men locked in silence. The exquisite colors of the sky began to slowly deepen. The trees around us were mostly maples. The light green of their new leaves, glistening on the branches as the breeze stirred them, seemed to grow gradually darker. The rumble of a cart sounded from a distant street. I imagined a fellow from the village had loaded it with shrubs or other such wares and was headed for a fair. Sensei rose abruptly at the sound of the cart, like a man called back from distant reveries.

"Shall we be going? The days are getting longer, but we've whiled this one away. The sun will set before we know it."

Sensei's backside betrayed his earlier nap on the platform. I brushed it clean with both hands.

"Thank you. Did I pick up any resin?"

"No, everything's gone."

"I just got this haori. The wife will be cross if I go and soil it already."

On our way back down the gently sloping hill, we approached the house again. Out on the veranda, which had been deserted on our way in, was the lady of the house with her daughter, a girl of fifteen or sixteen, who was helping her spool thread. From beside the gold fish basin we called out our thanks for their hospitality. The lady called back that we needn't mention it, and she thanked us as well for the nickel coin given to the boy.

When we'd made our way out the gate and walked for a while, I turned to Sensei and spoke. "Tell me, when you said earlier that any man, in the moment of truth, may emerge as a villain, what did you mean by it?"

"There's nothing profound there.—It's simply a fact. It's not a product of theory or reason."

"Granted it may be a fact, what I want to know is what you meant by moment of truth. To what sort of moment were you referring?"

Sensei laughed. It seemed that now, when the passion had left him, he had little interest in expounding. "I was referring to money. At the sight of money, the noblest of gentlemen unmasks his inner villain."

Sensei's answer left me dissatisfied. I sensed he was brushing me off, and I felt diminished. Feigning indifference, I set off walking at a quick pace. Sensei, in due course, began to fall behind. He called to me to wait.

"Look at that now."

"At what?"

"Your demeanor. Did I not just affect it with a single response?" I had stopped and turned to wait for him. He looked at my face as he said this.

Chapter 30

Deep down, in that moment, I hated Sensei. Even as we walked together again, shoulders side by side, I refrained from giving voice to the questions in my mind. Sensei, for his part, whether he noticed or not, showed not the slightest concern. As he ambled on with his easy gait and signature reticence, I grew more and more spiteful. I wanted to somehow get under his skin.

"Sensei."

"Yes?"

"You were a little worked up back there in the gardens. I've seldom ever seen you like that. Were you showing another side of yourself?"

Sensei made no immediate reply. I thought maybe I'd gotten to him. I also feared that maybe I'd missed the mark. At any rate, I decided to leave it at that. Sensei suddenly stepped to the side of the road, tucked up his shirttails, and relieved himself at the base of a neatly-trimmed hedge. I stood by idly as he finished his business.

"Pardon the delay."

With that he started walking again. I gave up at this point on arguing him into a corner. The road we were walking gradually came to life. The hills and valleys, with their wide cultivated fields, disappeared from view as houses closed in on both sides. Even still, the neighborhoods were quiet, and in some of the yards we saw peas climbing bamboo trelliswork, or chickens penned in by wire screen. A succession of cart horses, returning from the city center, approached and passed us by. Such sights were wont to grab my attention, and the questions that had occupied my thoughts were soon forgotten. When Sensei suddenly resurfaced our earlier exchange, it hit me as out of the blue.

"Did I really seem worked up back there?"

"Yes, a bit I suppose, but. . ."

"No, that's fine if I did. I was worked up. Discussions on wealth most easily set me off. You may not know it, but I'm terribly vindictive. I never forget a disgrace suffered or an injustice perpetrated. Ten years may pass, or even twenty, yet it all stays with me."

Sensei spoke with even more passion than before. What surprised me most, though, was not the passion in his words, but the meaning of what he said. I had certainly never expected to hear such revelations from him first hand, and I had never imagined him to harbor such tenacity. I'd believed him a meek spirit. His meekness and decency were what endeared him to me. In a fit of anger I'd challenged him, and now his words appalled me. He continued on.

"I was deceived. What's worse, I was deceived by my those of my own blood. I'll never forget it. While my father was alive, they had all seemed models of decency. However, the moment he died they began to reveal themselves—a pack of despicable rogues. The disgrace and injustice, all that I suffered at their hands, I've carried with me from my youth to this day. I expect I'll carry it forever. Only death can erase it from my mind. Nevertheless, I've yet to take my vengeance. Or then again, maybe it's no longer personal. I've already taken it further. I've come to despise the whole of humanity, of which those rogues are a part. I suppose that's enough."

I had no words of consolation to offer.

Chapter 31

Our conversation that day progressed no further. Unsettled by Sensei's demeanor, I was happy to let matters lie.

We boarded a train on the outskirts of the city, and once on board we hardly spoke. Shortly after disembarking, it was time to head our separate ways. As we parted, Sensei's mood seemed again to have changed. He said to me, in a tone much brighter than usual, "You're carefree from now until June. It's possible such days will never come again. Enjoy this time to the fullest."

I smiled in return and removed my cap. In doing so I looked at Sensei. Could such a man really, in the depths of his heart, harbor contempt for all humankind? His countenance betrayed not the slightest hint of such thoughts.

I must admit that I benefited greatly from my frequent discourse with Sensei. I should also say, though, that there were times when it left me hollow. I was left, on occasion, hanging in the dark. Our discussion that day in the country was one such example that sticks in my mind.

Not one to hold things back, I once divulged this to Sensei. Sensei laughed. I explained myself. "I wouldn't mind if I thought you incapable of elucidating. What bothers me is when you know the full story yet refuse to bring me along."

"I don't keep things from you."

"You do."

"I believe you're confusing my thoughts and ideas with my past experience. I may be a poor thinker, but what thoughts I have I freely share. There's no reason not to. Revealing my life to you in full detail, however, is an entirely different matter."

"It's not a different matter. Your thoughts are the products of your experience, which is why I hold them so dear. There's no value in one without the other. What can I gain from talk from an empty shell?"

Sensei, seemingly exasperated, looked me in the eye. The hand that held his cigarette trembled slightly. "You don't mince words."

"I'm simply sincere. I sincerely wish to know about life."

"Even if it means unearthing my past?"

The word "unearth" suddenly rang ominous in my ears. The man sitting before me, it seemed, was no longer Sensei, whom I'd come to respect, but an unknown malefactor. Sensei's face had gone pale.

"Are you truly sincere?" he pressed me again. "My past has left me distrustful of all, including even you. You're the one person, however, whom I don't want to doubt. Your innocence doesn't warrant distrust. I'd like to confide in someone, just one person is fine, before I die. Can you be that person? Will you be that for me? Are you sincere to the core of your being?"

"As my life is sincere, so too are my words." My voice quavered.

"Very well then," Sensei continued, "I'll tell you. I'll relate my past with no omission. If I do so. . . no, that doesn't matter. Bear in mind, though, that my story may not serve you. In the end, you may wish you hadn't sought it. Also—understand that I can't do this now. I'll relate it all in good time, but not until then."

Even after I returned to my lodgings, Sensei's words continued to weigh on me.

Chapter 32

My professors, it seemed, did not share my enthusiasm for my thesis. Nevertheless, I did receive passing marks. On graduation day, I pulled my musty old winter clothes from the trunk and put them on. As we lined up in the hall, all the faces showed signs of swelter. My body, sealed tight under thick wool, roasted intolerably. After a short while standing there, the handkerchief in my hand was sopped.

As soon as the ceremony ended, I returned to my room and stripped down. I opened the second floor window and surveyed the world through my diploma, which was rolled up tight like a spyglass. Then I tossed it onto my desk and sprawled myself out in the middle of the room. Lying there, I thought about my past. Then I imagined my future. That diploma, which stood like a sentinel between past and future, struck me as an odd piece of paper, in some ways profound and in some ways meaningless.

Sensei had invited me to dinner that night. We'd had a long-standing agreement that I would dine with him on the day of my graduation.

As promised, a table had been laid out in the parlor, near the veranda. A thick, embroidered tablecloth, stiffly starched, beautifully reflected the light of electric lamps. Whenever one dined at Sensei's, the dishes and utensils were set over white linen, the kind one finds in a Western-style restaurant. The linen was always freshly laundered, spotless, and pure white.

"Just like collars and cuffs. If you can't keep them clean, then don't choose white in the first place. White must be white."

This reminded me how fastidious Sensei was. His study, too, was always neatly arranged. As a careless man myself, I was often struck by the sharp contrast between us.

I'd once remarked to Sensei's wife how meticulous he was. She'd pointed out that he was not so meticulous when it came to his attire.

Sensei, who was listening nearby, had added with a grin, "To tell the truth, I'm psychologically meticulous. That's why I always suffer so. It really is an absurd condition."

It was unclear to me what he meant by "psychologically meticulous." Did he just mean that he was fussy in the common sense of the word, or did he mean that he was morally unrelenting? His wife, too, seemed unsure of his meaning.

That evening, I sat opposite Sensei with the signature white tablecloth before us. Sensei's wife sat between us, one on either side, with a direct view of the garden.

"Congratulations." Sensei raise his saké cup in my honor. I felt little sense of joy at this gesture. One reason, of course, was that there was scant joy in my heart for this word to unleash. At the same time, Sensei's manner of speaking instilled none either. There was nothing in his voice that lifted my spirits. He smiled as he raised his cup, and while there was no trace of ill temper or irony in his smile, there was also no sign of sincere happiness. His smile merely conveyed the fact that in this situation, this is what people are wont to do.

"It's splendid," Sensei's wife said to me, "your mother and father must be quite proud."

I suddenly thought of my father and his illness. I thought that I should go to him soon and present my diploma.

"Where does Sensei keep his diploma?" I asked.

"Where did we put it?—Do we still have it somewhere?" Sensei asked his wife.

"Yes, I believe we've saved it somewhere."

Neither seemed to know where it was.

Chapter 33

When it was time to eat, Sensei's wife sent the maidservant, who'd been seated at her side, off to the next room and proceeded to serve us herself. This, it seemed, was standard practice at Sensei's house with casual guests. I'd been uncomfortable with it at first, but now, after a number of occasions, I'd grown fully accustomed to being served in such manner.

"More tea? More rice? You're quite an eater." Sensei's wife had never been shy in commenting on my eating habits.

This day, however, on account of the heat, my appetite failed to impress.

"Done already? You've become such a light eater lately."

"I haven't become a light eater. It's just this hot weather."

After calling back the maidservant to clear the table, she next had ice cream and desert fruits served.

"We prepared this ourselves."

Sensei's wife, who was not so busy with household chores, had the time to make ice cream for her guests. I asked for seconds.

"Now that you've graduated, what do you plan to do next?" Sensei asked. Sensei had shifted his seat halfway onto the veranda and was leaning his back against the open shōji.

I'd been focused on graduation and given no thought as to what was next. Seeing my hesitation, Sensei's wife asked if I might take a teaching position. When I still didn't answer, she suggested the civil service. Sensei and I both laughed.

"To tell the truth, I have no idea. I've hardly given a thought to taking an occupation. I'm not sure how one choses. With no experience to draw on, it's hard to know what best to do."

"That may be true. However, it's your family's wealth that affords you such leisure. Look at those who are pinched. I would doubt they're as unconcerned as yourself."

Some of my friends had secured middle school teaching positions well in advance of graduation. Deep down, I knew that Sensei's wife was right. However, I replied with, "A bit of Sensei must have rubbed off on me."

"Well, don't let it be more than a bit."

Sensei forced a smile. "No harm if it does rub off, just remember what I told you the other day. While your father's still with you, arrange for your share of his wealth. Until you've done so, you mustn't rest easy."

I recalled that day in early May, when Sensei and I had ventured out of the city and into the vast gardens of the nursery, where azaleas were in bloom. On our way home, Sensei had become quite worked up. I replayed in my mind the forceful words he'd directed my way. They had, on second thought, rang more dire than forceful. At the same time, however, I did not know what was behind them, and they'd failed to move me.

"Tell me, how much money do you and Sensei have?"

"Why would you ask such a thing?"

"Because Sensei refuses to tell me."

She smiled and looked at Sensei. "Probably because there's nothing worth telling."

"But I'd like to know what it takes to live like Sensei. Do tell me, so when I speak with my father I can know what I'm after."

Sensei had turned toward the garden and was smoking with an air of detachment. My only recourse was to continue with his wife.

"It's not enough to even make mention of. We find a way to get by as we are.—At any rate, you really must apply yourself to something. Just idling about like Sensei is out of the question. . ."

"I don't just idle about." Sensei turned his head to challenge his wife's words.

Chapter 34

It was after ten when I left Sensei's place. In several days I would return to the country, so before getting up from the table I offered parting words.

"I won't see you again for some time."

"Will you be back in September?" Sensei's wife asked.

Now that I'd graduated, there was no particular need for me to return in September. I was sure, though, that I was not going to spend the dog days of August in Tōkyō. Nor was I compelled to come back early to seek a position.

"I suppose around September."

"Well, take care then. We may do some traveling this summer ourselves. It looks to be hot here this year. If we do go, we'll send you a postcard."

"Where did you have in mind?"

Sensei was grinning as he listened to this exchange. "We don't even know yet that we're going."

Sensei suddenly stopped me as I prepared to rise from my seat. "By the way, how is your father's health?" he asked.

There'd been no updates on my father's health. No news, I'd figured, was good news.

"It's a serious condition. Renal failure is the end of the road."

I'd never heard the term "renal failure," and I had no idea what it meant. Back home during winter break, when we'd talked with the doctor, he hadn't voiced any such term.

"Do take good care of him," Sensei's wife added, "Once the poison reaches his brain, you've lost him. It really is serious."

I had no experience in such things, and I floated an awkward grin to mask my disquietude. "His disease, they tell us, is incurable, so we'll just have to take things as they come."

"As long as you're resigned to what's coming."

Sensei's wife, perhaps thinking back on her own mother's death from the same disease, spoke in a subdued tone and then shifted her gaze downward. I felt truly sorry for my father and the fate that awaited him.

At this point, Sensei turned to his wife and asked, "Shizu, do you think you'll die before I do?"

"Why?"

"I was just wondering. Or do you think I'll go first? That's usually the case. The husband goes first and the wife is left behind."

"Not necessarily. It's just because husbands tend to be older."

"That's why the husband goes first then. Which means I'm bound to depart this world before you do."

"You're the exception."

"You think so?"

"You're fit as a fiddle. When have you ever been truly ill? I'm quite sure I'll go first."

"Really?"

"Yes, I believe so."

Sensei looked at me. I smiled in return.

"Suppose I do go first. What will you do?"

"What will I. . ."

Her speech faltered. The idea of Sensei's death, and the thought of her own sorrow, seemed to upset her. When she raised her eyes again, however, she'd regained her composure.

"After all, what can I do? Through thick and thin one rolls with the punches."

She shot me a knowing look as she answered him tongue-in-cheek.

Chapter 35

I'd been preparing to take my leave but instead made myself comfortable again. I didn't want to disrupt the conversation.

"What do you think?" Sensei asked me.

I had never, of course, given any thought to who would die first, Sensei or his wife. All I could do was laugh. "Don't look to me to tell you the number of your days."

"It really is about numbered days, isn't it? Each of us is born with a given amount, no more and no less. Sensei's mother and father, for example, departed this world nearly together."

"They both died on the same day?"

"Not the same day, but close to it. One after the other." This was news to me. I was intrigued.

"How did they manage that?"

Sensei interrupted his wife before she could answer. "Let's not get into that. It's of no relevance."

Sensei held a fan in his hand, and he made a point of stirring the air with it. Then he turned back to his wife, "Shizu, after I'm gone this house will be yours."

She smiled. "How about the land it's on too?"

"I'm afraid the land's not mine to give, but all my possessions will be yours."

"That's fine, but what do I do with all those foreign books?"

"Sell them to a dealer."

"How much are they worth?"

Sensei didn't answer her question. However, he remained fixated on the distant subject of his own death. He seemed convinced that his own death would precede his wife's. His wife, initially, made her best effort to take the discussion in stride. As it went on, though, the subject began to weigh on her feminine sensibilities.

"After I'm gone... After I'm gone... How many times have you said that? For Heaven's sake, please stop already. You're only inviting misfortune. If such time should come, you can rest assured that all will be handled according to your wishes. Isn't that enough?"

Sensei turned toward the garden with a grin. However, in deference to his wife he spoke no more on this subject. Not wanting to overstay my welcome, I immediately rose from my seat. Sensei and his wife saw me to the entry hall together.

"Take good care of your father," Sensei's wife told me.

"We'll see you in September," Sensei added.

I acknowledged their salutations and stepped out through the latticed door. Between the entryway and the gate stood a single fragrant olive tree. In the darkness, it seemed to be stretching its limbs to block my way. Taking several steps toward it, I surveyed its dark, densely foliated branch-ends, and I imagined the flowers and fragrances of the autumn to come. This olive tree and Sensei's house, from my earliest memories of them, were inseparable in my mind. As I stood before the tree, thinking ahead to someday in autumn when I'd next cross Sensei's threshold, the light that had spilled from the entry hall went out. Sensei and his wife, it seemed, had retired to their inner rooms. I went out alone onto the dark street.

I didn't return directly to my lodgings. I needed to buy things for my trip home, and my stomach needed a chance to settle, so I walked toward the lights of the town, where the evening was still young. In the mass of men and women milling about, I ran across a fellow graduate. He pulled me into a bar, determined that I drink with him. Once there, I was subjected to his bluster, which the froth on my beer easily exceeded in substance. I didn't get back to my lodgings till after twelve.

Chapter 36

The following day I again braved the heat to go and buy what I needed. I'd received a letter listing requested items, and I'd thought little of it at the time, but it struck me now as a terrible imposition. As I mopped my brow on the train, I felt growing spite for the folks back home. Did they even appreciate their demands on my time and the effort involved?

I had no intention of merely whiling away the summer. I'd drafted up a work plan for my days back home, and in order to execute this plan there were books I had to buy. I committed myself to half a day on the second floor of Maruzen. I found the shelves that housed the books in my field of interest, and I examined each offering one by one.

In the course my shopping, what taxed me most was a decorative collar for a woman's kimono. The shop clerk was happy to show me an assortment of wares, but when came to deciding, I struggled. Furthermore, the pricing seemed arbitrary. I would ask about one that looked affordable, and find it was far too expensive. I'd avoid others that looked too refined, and they'd turn out to be modestly priced. When I compared several side by side, there was nothing to justify the difference in price. I was completely confounded. Inwardly, I kicked myself now for not having gone to Sensei's wife.

I bought a bag. It was, of course, an inferior piece of domestic make, but its shiny clasps would impress the folks back home. I bought it at my mother's behest. She had instructed me in her letter to buy myself a new bag when I graduated. I was then to fill it with her requested items. I'd laughed when I'd read this. I could understand her thinking, but somehow it all struck me as comical.

Just as I'd announced to Sensei and his wife in parting, I boarded a train three days hence to depart from Tōkyō and journey home. Since the prior winter, Sensei had offered considerable counsel on my father's illness. While I had every reason to feel concern, I found myself, in contrast, remarkably subdued. I was troubled most by thoughts of my mother alone after his death. In my mind, no doubt, I had already come to terms with my father's mortality. In a letter to my elder brother in Kyūshū, I had stated plainly that Father would never recover his health. I had also urged him to find time this summer, despite his duties, to visit home and look one last time into Father's eyes. In an appeal to his sentiment, I'd added that it would be unconscionable for us, as children, to leave our aged parents forsaken and forlorn in the country. These words, as I wrote them, were sincere and from the heart. Afterward, however, they seemed to ring hollow.

I reflected on this contradiction as I sat in the train. As I reflected, I came to see myself as fickle and superficial. I felt dissatisfied. I turned my thoughts to Sensei and his wife. In particular, I thought back on that conversation at their dinner table.

"Which of us do you suppose will die first?"

I silently repeated the question that Sensei and his wife had considered that evening. I knew full well that such a question could never be answered with any certainty. But what if it could? What if they did know who was to die first? What would Sensei do? What would Sensei's wife do? I wondered what they could do, other than carry on just as they were. (Just as I, with the death of my father back home approaching, also carried on.) Human life, I saw, was something fleeting. Our drive to persevere, to carry on with a brave face, I also saw as hollow and fleeting.

BOOK TWO
MY PARENTS AND I

Chapter 1

What struck me on returning home was how little my father's health had changed in my absence.

"Welcome home. So, you've graduated. Splendid. Give me a moment to go wash up."

Father had been doing something in the garden. He was wearing an old straw hat with a soiled handkerchief tied behind to block the sun. The handkerchief flapped as he hurried round back to the well.

To me, graduation was nothing special. It was what one did as a matter of course. Father's elation caught me off guard.

"You've graduated. Splendid."

He repeated this time and again. In my mind, I compared my father's elation with Sensei's expression as he'd toasted me that night at his dinner table after the ceremony. Sensei, who'd outwardly cheered my graduation while inwardly disparaging it, seemed nobler somehow than my father, who was overly pleased by something mundane. I began to fault him for his provincialism.

"A university graduation is nothing all that splendid. Hundreds graduate each year."

When I finally voiced my thoughts, he looked at me in an odd way.

"It's not just your graduation I'm calling splendid. Your graduation, no doubt, is splendid enough, but there's more to my words than just that. If you'd see things once from my perspective. . ."

I tried to ask what he meant, but he was reluctant to continue. After a bit, he finally went on.

"Let me tell you what's splendid. You're aware that my health is failing me. When you were home last winter, I wondered if I'd last even three or four more months. By whatever good fortune, I'm still here today in sound mind and of able body. And now you've graduated. What more could I wish for? Can you not indulge the joy of a parent at being alive, rather than dead, for his son's hard-won graduation? I know you have grand plans, and I know your graduation is only the start, so I suppose my fussing annoys you. Imagine yourself in my shoes, though. Things are quite different. Your graduation is far more splendid to me than it is to you. Can you understand that?"

There was nothing I could say. Too ashamed to even apologize, I merely hung my head. My father had been calmly resigned to his own death. He had convinced himself, it seems, that he wouldn't live to see me graduate. I'd been too far the fool to see what my graduation meant to him. I took my diploma from my bag and presented it to my parents with due respect. Something in the bag had bent it out of shape. My father carefully unrolled it.

"A thing like this should be kept rolled and hand carried."

"You should have set something in the center," my mother advised.

After examining the diploma for a time, my father rose and carried it to the alcove, where he placed it in prominent view for all to see. I refrained from voicing my usual objections. I had no intention any more of defying my parents. I let my father do as he pleased. The damaged parchment, though, had a mind of its own. As soon as it set in place, it wanted to pull in on itself and topple over.

Chapter 2

I took my mother aside to ask after my father's condition.

"Father was out in the garden. Are you sure it's okay?"

"He seems fine these days. I suppose, perhaps, he's recovering."

I was surprised how she took things in stride. Like any woman living a quiet life in the country, she was utterly uninformed in such matters. Even so, I struggled to reconcile her current calm with her anxious fretting in those days after Father's initial bout.

"But didn't the doctor pronounce his condition grave?"

"The human body, it would seem, is truly a wondrous thing. Despite the doctor's solemn words, your father's still going and active on his feet. I was worried at first, and I did my best to keep him in bed, but you know how he is. He tries not to overdo it, but he's stubborn in his ways. Since he's convinced he's okay, he has no more mind to heed me."

I recalled Father's behavior on the occasion of my previous visit. He'd forced himself out of bed and shaved, telling me the while that he was fine, and that Mother was making much ado of nothing. It wouldn't be fair to reproach my mother on his account. I wanted to tell her to at least caution him, but in the end I held my silence. I did explain to her all that I knew of the nature of Father's illness. Most of this was from Sensei and his wife. Mother didn't seem particularly moved by this new information. She merely nodded, expressed pity, and asked how old the deceased had been.

The only thing to do, I decided, was to talk to Father directly. He listened more receptively to my counsel than my mother had.

"No doubt, no doubt. You're absolutely correct. However, at the end of the day it's my body, and over the years I've come to know it well. More than anyone else, I believe I know its limitations and its needs."

My mother listened with a wry smile. "See what I mean?" she said.

"Even so, Father's resolved himself to what's coming. That's why he was so pleased to see me graduate and return home with my diploma. He told me himself he didn't think he'd live to see the day, much less still have his health."

"Don't be fooled by what he says. Deep down, he knows he still has time."

"You really think so?"

"He intends to keep on. Maybe for ten years, maybe for twenty. Granted, he does worry me at times. He tells me he doesn't have long. Then he asks what I'll do when he's gone, if I can manage alone."

I suddenly imagined my mother, minus my father, in this big old country house. Could she run things herself with Father gone? What would my elder brother do? What would Mother's wishes be? In light of all that, could I leave this place for a comfortable existence in Tōkyō? As thoughts of Mother filled my mind, I also recalled what Sensei had said—if there's property involved, receive your due share now, while your father is still of sound mind and body.

"Not to worry. The ones who say they're dying never do. Who knows how many years he'll go on, pronouncing his own demise all the while. It's the healthy ones, with nothing to complain of, who end up going first."

I listened in silence to my mother's clichéd remark, defensible by neither rational thought nor statistical evidence.

Chapter 3

Mother and Father began to talk about inviting guests for a red-rice banquet in my honor. From the day of my return, I'd been secretly dreading such a thing. I immediately begged off.

"Please, you mustn't go to any great lengths."

I hated these country guests. Their purpose in coming, betrayed by their behavior, was solely food and drink, never mind the occasion. Even from my childhood, I'd cringed at the thought of serving them at our table. Far worse this time, they'd be coming on my account. I couldn't tell my parents point blank to dispense with this vulgar horde. All I could do was insist that they shouldn't put themselves out.

"But we're not putting ourselves out. Not in the least. How many times will our son graduate from college? Don't be so modest—it's only natural to celebrate."

My mother took great pride in my graduation. To her, it was no less an occasion than marriage.

"We don't have to invite guests, but if we don't then folks will talk."

This was my father's view. He was concerned what people might say. It was indeed true that, on occasions such as this, unmet expectations would invariably lead to whispers among the neighbors.

"It's not like Tōkyō. Folks around here are set in their ways."

"Your father has his reputation to consider," my mother added.

I could argue my case no further. I decided to let them do as they best saw fit.

"I only meant that you shouldn't go to great lengths on my account. If you need to placate the neighbors to stop their grumbling, then that's another matter. Far be it for me to assert myself and put you in arrears."

"Don't get so cynical on us." Father looked annoyed.

"Father never said it wasn't on your account, but I trust you have at least some inkling of what societal obligation means."

Mother pitched in her usual measure of female incoherence. In the same vein, she could easily outtalk both Father and I combined.

"You educate a man and he comes back a cynic."

Father said no more. However, in this single remark he'd laid bare his long-standing resentment. At the time, I was oblivious to my own abrasive manner. I saw myself only as a victim of unfair judgments.

That evening, in a quieter mood, Father asked my preferences, if we were to invite guests, for a date. He knew full well that I was biding time in that old house, and any day was as good as the next. Asking my preferences was a conciliatory gesture on his part. In response, I lowered my head in deference. We talked together and settled on a date.

As we awaited our chosen date, momentous news arrived. It was announced that Emperor Meiji had fallen ill. News of this happening, which the papers immediately proclaimed to the nation, hit our country house and blew asunder the plans for my party, those plans that we'd worked so to settle.

"Well, I guess we'd better hold off," Father said as he perused the paper through his reading glasses. He seemed to also be reflecting on his own health.

I thought back to my recent graduation, and how the Emperor had honored the occasion with his customary appearance.

Chapter 4

In the quiet of that old house, which was far too large for the few of us there, I unpacked my bags and began to tackle my texts. For whatever reason, I struggled to concentrate. In that second floor room of my lodgings in Tōkyō, where the great city had clamored and the rattle of distant trains had filled my ears, I'd matched the vigor of my surroundings, plowing my way through page after page.

I caught myself readily dozing at my desk. At times, I would even grab a pillow and indulge in a full-fledged nap. On waking, the sounds of cicadas filled my ears. Their chirping, which carried like a call from the greater world outside, would suddenly overwhelm me. I'd listen intently, sometimes struck by a feeling of loneliness.

I took up my pen and wrote to various friends. To some I penned brief postcards, to others lengthy letters. Some of these friends were still in Tōkyō. Others had returned to far away homes. Some wrote back, and others I didn't hear from. I didn't forget Sensei, of course. I decided to tell him all that had happened since my return home, and I filled three pages with small print in the process. As I sealed the envelope, I wondered whether Sensei was even still in Tōkyō. When Sensei left home with his wife, he always had the same woman tend his house. She looked to be fifty or so, and she wore her hair loose in the style of a widow. I'd once asked Sensei about her, and he'd asked in return who I thought her to be. I'd assumed, incorrectly it turned out, that she was one of his relatives. Sensei informed me that he had no relatives. He'd severed all contact with remaining relations back home. The woman I'd asked about, who tended his house, was of no connection to Sensei. She was a relative on his wife's side. As I posted my letter, I suddenly called her to mind, her narrow kimono sash tied comfortably in back. I wondered, should my letter arrive while Sensei and his wife were away for the summer, if this elderly widow would have the foresight and consideration to forward it on to them. I knew full well, of course, that there was nothing in it to warrant such handling. I was simply lonesome and hoping for a return letter from Sensei. None arrived.

Unlike during my home time the previous winter, Father this time was uninterested in shōgi. The shōgi board had been set aside in a corner of the alcove, and it remained there gathering dust. Especially since the Emperor's illness, Father seemed lost in his own thoughts. Each day he waited on the newspaper, and each day he read it first off. When done, he would seek me out, paper still in hand.

"Take a look. There's lots again on His Highness."

Father always referred to the Emperor as His Highness.

"It may be presumptuous of me, but I believe His Highness and I are suffering from the same thing."

As he spoke, a dark shadow of concern clouded his features. I felt anxious myself at his words, wondering when he might next be forced off his feet.

"He'll be alright, though. If a common man like myself can manage. . ."

Even as he sought to reassure himself, his words fell heavy with an imminent sense of foreboding.

"Father really fears for his health," I told my mother. "He doesn't share your confidence in ten or twenty more years."

Mother seemed at a loss.

"See if he'll play shōgi with you."

I pulled the shōgi board from the alcove and dusted it off.

Chapter 5

Father's health slowly deteriorated. His old straw hat with the handkerchief tied behind, the one I'd been alarmed to see him putter around in, in due course fell out of use. When I saw that hat sitting idle on the soot-darkened shelf, I felt pity for my father. Before, when he'd move about easily, I'd worried he was overtaxing himself. Now that he sat quietly, I felt he'd been right in keeping active. I often discussed Father's health with my mother.

"It's all in his head," my mother remarked. She believed Father's suffering was sympathetic, in deference to the Emperor.

"It's not in his head. Do you believe he's really not ailing? I think he's wearing a brave face in spite of his physical failing."

As I answered, I was thinking to myself that I might call the specialist back to examine him.

"I'm afraid this summer's been a disappointment for you. You've graduated from the university, yet there's no celebration. Your father's in such a state, and then there's the Emperor.—We should have summoned guests immediately on your return."

I'd returned around the fifth of July. A week later, my mother and father had started talking about inviting guests to celebrate my graduation. When we'd finally settled on a date, it was another week and some days further out. From my perspective, the leisurely pace of country life, unfettered by time, had spared me the pain of unpleasant company. My mother still had no idea how I saw things.

When news of the Emperor's death arrived, my father held the newspaper in his hands and let out a sigh.

"It's happened. His Highness is gone. I suppose. . ."

He didn't finish his thought.

I went to town for some black silk. I wrapped the ball on the end of the flag pole, tied a trailing strip just below it, and mounted the pole on the gateway pillar angled out toward the road. Both flag and black strip hung loosely in the still air. The roof over that gateway of our old house was thatched in straw. Wind and rain had buffeted the straw over time and faded its color. It was now tinged an ashen gray and was noticeably uneven in places. From outside the gate, I surveyed the black strip and the white woolen flag with its red-dyed sun circle. I also viewed them against the weathered straw of the gateway roof. I recalled how Sensei had once asked me about the construction of our house, wondering if it differed much from the houses in his own home town. I'd wished I could show him this house where I'd been born. At the same time, I'd feared I might feel shame in doing so.

I went back inside. Returning to the room where my desk was, I read the paper and let my thoughts drift off toward Tōkyō. I conjured in my mind an image of the great metropolis. I imagined it dark and somber, yet fluid with restless motion. In that city that couldn't stay still, that was steeped in anxiety, I imagined Sensei's house as a fixed point of light. I was yet unaware that this light would be swallowed in a silent maelstrom, that this lamp was confronting its fate and was soon to shine no more.

I took up my pen to update Sensei on recent events. I wrote ten lines and then stopped. I tore up my draft and tossed it into the trash. (There was no point writing such things to Sensei, and there was no reason to think that this time he'd write me back.) I felt forlorn. That was why I wrote. I was holding out hope for an answer.

Chapter 6

In mid-August a letter arrived from a friend. In it, he mentioned an instructor's post at a provincial middle school and asked if I was interested. This friend, spurred by financial necessity, had been seeking such a position. When this offer had come to him, he'd already settled on something more favorable. Hence he'd been considerate enough to write and recommend it to me in turn. I immediately wrote back and declined. An acquaintance of mine was struggling to secure a teaching post. I suggested this fellow would likely be receptive to the offer.

After sending off my reply, I informed my parents. They seemed to have no objection to my declining the offer.

"There must certainly be better positions that aren't so remote."

Behind these words, I could sense they harbored great expectations for my future. Uninformed as they were, they anticipated that renown and fortune awaited me now that I'd graduated.

"Good positions are hard to come by these days. Things have changed since my brother's time, and our areas of expertise are different. You mustn't assume a similar outcome."

"With degree in hand, though, you need to at least establish yourself. What will I say when people ask after my second son and what he's made of himself after graduating?"

Father made a sour face. With no experience in the broader world, he was fully provincial in his thinking. The local folk were bound to ask about me. They'd want to know how much a university graduate earned, whether it topped a hundred yen. If I didn't arm him with a sound answer, his repute would suffer. My own thinking had been shaped by the big city and was fully alien to that of my parents. No doubt they saw me as an odd species, like a being that walked with its legs skyward. For my part, I sometimes felt I was such a creature. The gulf between us was so wide that I largely refrained from sharing my thoughts.

"What about that man you call Sensei? If ever he's going to help you, then isn't this the time?"

This was the extent of Mother's understanding of Sensei. The same Sensei who, on my return home to the country, had urged me to receive my share of the family wealth while Father still lived. Brokering a position for me on my graduation was hardly within his purview.

"What was it that he does?" Father asked.

"He has no occupation," I answered.

I'd told my parents from the start that Sensei was not employed. My father, I expect, had not forgotten.

"How can he not be employed? He must do something to have earned your admiration so."

Father was goading me. The way he saw things, any man of worth should have established himself in the world in a position of respect. A man of leisure, it thus followed, could be nothing but a wastrel.

"I don't earn a paycheck myself, but I try to at least keep busy," Father continued.

I held my tongue.

"If he's the distinguished gentleman you describe him as, then certainly he can find you something. Have you tried asking him?"

"I haven't," I answered.

"You won't know if you don't try. Why not ask him? Write to him at least."

"Okay."

I returned a reluctant response and rose from my seat.

Chapter 7

Father was clearly apprehensive about his health. However, he was not one to pester the doctor with pointless questions. The doctor, for his part, refrained from belaboring the situation.

Father, it seemed, was considering our lives without him. At the very least, he was considering the fate of his household.

"Educating one's children is both good and bad. You work to provide them with schooling, and it's guaranteed they won't stay home. Higher learning is an expedient for dissolving one's family."

My older brother's education had drawn him far away. The result of my own education was a firm resolve to reside in Tōkyō. Father's grumblings on this account were not unjustified. The idea of my mother left alone in this old country house to fend for herself clearly unsettled him.

Father firmly believed that his household was rooted in place. He also believed that my mother would remain there for all of her days. He worried greatly for her, left alone to care for the large house without him. At the same time, he urged me to secure a prominent position in Tōkyō. His inconsistency afforded me the chance to return to Tōkyō, and for this I was grateful.

Before my parents, I did my best to feign an effort at securing a prominent post. I wrote to Sensei and explained the situation at home. I asked if he couldn't, through his connections, mediate any sort of position on my behalf. Even as I penned my request, I didn't expect he would act. Even if he wanted to, I thought as I wrote, he had no network to draw on. I did expect, however, that this letter must certainly merit a response.

Before sealing and posting it, I turned to my mother and offered, "I've written to Sensei, just as you suggested. Give it a look."

As I'd imagined, she declined.

"If it's ready then post it without delay. You should have done so sooner, without folks having to prompt you."

Mother still regarded me as a child. And I felt, in fact, like I was still a child.

"A simple letter, you know, won't suffice. Come September or so, I'll need to travel to Tōkyō."

"I suppose so, but you never know that there might not be some chance just waiting. The sooner you get your request in the better."

"Agreed. Anyway, an answer is sure to arrive. Once it does we can talk about next steps."

I had full faith in Sensei, who was always so meticulous in such matters. I looked forward to his response.

My expectations, however, were disappointed. A week went by with still no word.

"They must have gone off to escape the summer heat."

I felt compelled to offer some explanation, not just for my mother's sake, but for my own as well. To quell my concerns over Sensei, I conjured up circumstances to explain his behavior.

At times I forgot about Father's illness. All I would think of was getting back to Tōkyō. Father himself seemed to also forget he was ill. He was concerned for the future, but his concern induced no action. Time went by with no chance, as Sensei had advised, to talk through division of assets.

Chapter 8

In early September I was finally ready to return to Tōkyō. I went to my father and asked for a resumption of my educational stipend.

"Remaining here like this, I'll never secure the kind of position you've suggested."

I presented my return to Tōkyō as a quest to fulfill his expectations.

"Of course it's only until I find a position," I added.

Inwardly, I held little hope of procuring anything remarkable. My father, though, who had little knowledge of the ways of the world, saw things differently.

"I suppose we can manage for a while then. But don't let it be for too long. As soon as you've found a suitable post, you'll need to support yourself. In principle, the day you graduate should be the last day you rely on anyone else. Today's youth are well versed in spending but give no thought to earning."

Father voiced multiple grievances. Among them were statements like, "It used to be that children supported their parents, but today's children just take and take." I simply listened in silence.

When the airing of grievances came to an end, I quietly moved to rise from my seat. Father asked when I was planning to leave. From my perspective, sooner was better.

"Ask your mother to choose an auspicious day."

"I'll do that."

In those days I was uncharacteristically deferential toward my father. I hoped to take my leave without upsetting him. Father stopped me again.

"When you leave for Tōkyō, the house will be lonely again. At any rate, it'll just be your mother and me. It would be one thing if I were healthy, but in my current state there's no telling what may happen."

I did my best to console my father and then went back to where my desk was. Sitting among my scattered books, I replayed in my mind his forlorn look and rueful words. I heard again the chirping of the cicadas, but the sound was different than before. It was now the "tsuku-tsuku" sound of a different variety. Whenever I'd returned home in summertime and sat quietly among the seething sound of cicadas, I'd been often struck by a strange melancholy. It was a sorrow that, wrapped in the fervent cries of these insects, permeated my soul to its core. In such times I'd remain still and think back on my life.

This summer, the sorrows I'd felt since returning had gradually shifted in tone. Like the voices of different cicadas, one giving way to the next, I pictured the fates of those who were close to me, steadily treading a grand cycle of death and rebirth. While reflecting on the lonely words and lonely look of my father, I also thought of Sensei, who had left my letters unanswered. The impressions in my mind of Sensei and my father were extreme opposites, but whether for purpose of comparison or through stream of consciousness, I would often think of them together.

I was intimately familiar with my father. If I saw him no more, then my regret would be merely that of a child missing a parent. Sensei was largely unknown to me still. He'd promised to share his past but had not yet done so. In short, he was a figure in the dark. I couldn't be content, I felt, until I'd pulled him into the light. The thought of losing him distressed me greatly. I consulted with my mother, and we chose a day for my departure for Tōkyō.

Chapter 9

As the day of my departure finally approached (I believe it was the evening two days prior) Father blacked out again. I was securing my baggage, which I'd packed full with books and clothing. Father had just gone in to bathe. My mother, who'd gone in to scrub his back, cried out for me in a loud voice. I went and saw my father, fully naked, supported from behind by my mother. By the time we got him back to the parlor, he was insisting again that all was fine. Out of caution, I stayed at his bedside and cooled his head with a damp washcloth. It was past nine when I finally finished a cursory dinner.

The next day, Father was in surprisingly good spirits. Despite our objections, he insisted on walking to the toilet unaided.

"I'm fine now."

Father repeated the same words he'd said to me after swooning late last year. At that time, true to his word, he really had seemed fine. I thought maybe this time might be the same. The doctor, however, could not be pressed to give any definitive prognosis. He simply advised an abundance of caution. The day of my departure came, but I was too unsettled to bring myself to leave.

"Maybe I should wait a bit and see how he's doing," I suggested to my mother.

"Yes, please do," she replied.

My mother, who had shown no concern before with Father puttering about in the garden or backyard, was now overly concerned and worrying herself sick.

"Weren't you leaving for Tōkyō today?" my father asked me.

"Yes, but I've put it off for a bit," I replied.

"On my account, I suppose?" he asked further.

I hesitated. If I answered yes, it would only confirm the gravity of his condition. I didn't want to set his nerves on edge. My father, though, could see what I was thinking.

"I'm sorry for this," he said as he gazed at the garden.

I went to my room and surveyed the baggage left lying there. It was tied up tightly, ready to be carried out at any moment. I stood before it, wondering vaguely if I should unpack.

I passed the next few days in a restless state, like one half risen from his seat. Then Father collapsed again.

The doctor ordered absolute rest.

"What do you think?" Mother asked me privately in a quiet voice, a look of discouragement on her face.

I was ready to send out telegrams to my brother and sister. However, Father seemed to be resting comfortably. From his speech and overall manner, one would hardly know he was ailing from more than a cold. On top of that, his appetite was voracious. We cautioned him, but to no avail.

"I don't have long anyway, so where's the harm in a little indulgence?"

I found his use of the word "indulgence" both amusing and, at the same time, in some way pathetic. Father had never lived in the big city, and he had no idea of true indulgence. In the evenings, he would have my mother grill rice cakes and chew them down greedily.

"What's behind these cravings? Somewhere inside, his body must still be sound."

My mother was pinning her hopes in thin air. At the same time, her use of the word "craving" all but acknowledged that Father was not his usual self.

My uncle came to visit, and only reluctantly did Father let him leave. Loneliness was the main reason, but he also believed himself underfed, and he was looking for a sympathetic ear.

Chapter 10

A week or more passed with no change in Father's condition. During that time, I wrote a long letter to my brother in Kyūshū and had my mother write to my sister. I was convinced that these were the last letters we'd write them concerning Father's health. We indicated in both letters that when the time came we would send word by telegram, on receipt of which they should come at once.

My brother was steeped in his work, and my sister was expecting a child, so neither could be called home unless the moment demanded it. At the same time, I dreaded the thought of them making the journey only to arrive too late. The decision on when to summon them was mine, and they couldn't know how heavily it weighed on me.

"I can't give you a definitive answer. All I can tell you is prepare yourselves. The critical stage could come any time now."

These were the words of the doctor whom I'd fetched from the station in town. I talked with my mother, and we decided to ask him to send us a nurse from the clinic. Father looked strangely at the woman in white who arrived at his bedside.

Father had known for some time that his illness was terminal. Even so, he had not yet acknowledged the actuality of death.

"When I'm better, I'll go see Tōkyō once more. One never knows the number of one's days. One has to act while one can."

"Take me with you when you go."

My mother had no choice but to humor him.

There were times too when he felt terribly despondent.

"After I'm gone, take good care of your mother for me."

The words "after I'm gone" were linked in my mind to another occasion. On the evening of the day of my graduation, prior to my departure from Tōkyō, Sensei had used these words repeatedly in conversation with his wife. I remembered the light grin on Sensei's face, and I remembered his wife's refusal to engage, warning him that he was only inviting misfortune. On that occasion, "after I'm gone" had been purely hypothetical. As I heard it now, it was imminently real. I couldn't brush it aside as Sensei's wife had done. All the same, I did what I could to take my father's mind off the matter.

"Don't let yourself get down. Didn't you say that as soon as you're better you'll go see Tōkyō? And that you'll take Mother too? You'll be amazed at all that's changed. There are new rail lines everywhere. Once a line comes through, the city transforms itself. Urban renewal programs are underway as well. In the course of a day, you won't see Tōkyō at rest for even a moment."

I may have felt compelled to say too much, but Father, for his part, listened appreciatively.

With an invalid in the house, a natural succession of visitors appeared. Nearby kinfolk would stop by in turn, one every day or two. There were also distant relatives whom we saw only rarely.

"We were wondering how he is. He seems all right. His speech is coherent, and his face is hardly gaunt."

With such remarks they would make their way back home. Our house, which upon my return had been quiet to a fault, grew livelier by the day with this traffic.

Father lay still in the center of it all, his condition slowly deteriorating. I consulted with my mother and uncle and finally wired my brother and sister. My brother replied that he'd come at once. My sister's husband also confirmed an immediate departure. My sister's previous pregnancy had ended in miscarriage, and her husband had informed us already that he thought to take no chances this time. We expected he might come alone in her place.

Chapter 11

In the midst of all this commotion, I could still sit quietly at times. On some occasions, I could open a book and read ten pages undisturbed. My baggage, once bound up so tightly, was by now fully undone. I took out various items as needed. I thought back to the goals I'd set for the summer on leaving Tōkyō. I hadn't achieved but a third of them. The discontent of such failure was nothing new to me. However, I'd rarely fallen so short as this past summer. I told myself such failures were typical, common to all men, but to little consolation.

Stewing in my displeasure, I thought on the one hand of my father's illness. I imagined our lives without him. At the same time, I thought on the other hand of Sensei. These two countenances, so different in their schooling, disposition, and social standing, bracketed my sour mood at both ends.

As I sat there, away from my father's bedside and off by myself among scattered books, with arms folded in front of me, my mother appeared.

"Why not rest for a bit? You must be worn out."

My mother did not understand what I was thinking. And I was not so naïve as to expect that she should. I merely thanked her. She remained in the doorway.

"How is Father?" I asked.

"He's sleeping soundly now," she answered.

To my surprise, she came in and sat at my side.

"Any word yet from Sensei?"

She'd placed her faith in me. I'd assured her that Sensei would write me back without fail. From the start, however, I'd never anticipated the kind of answer my parents were hoping for. As things now stood, it was as though I'd knowingly misled them.

"Why not try writing once more?"

I would gladly write any number of letters, even to no avail, for my mother's sake. However, the last thing I wanted to do was badger Sensei. Much more than my father's scolding or my mother's disappointment, I feared the loss of Sensei's respect. I was worried I might have perturbed him already, and hence his silence with respect to my request.

"It's easy enough to write a letter, but this isn't something one manages by post. I'll need to get to Tōkyō and do some legwork."

"True, but with your father's condition there's no telling when that might be."

"I'm not going anywhere anytime soon. Until we have an outcome, recovery or otherwise, I intend to stay right where I am."

"I'm afraid you'll have to. One can't leave a man in your father's state to go and roam round Tōkyō."

At first, I was sympathetic toward my mother and her lack of worldly experience. I couldn't understand, though, why she insisted on raising this subject again at this time. I wondered if it was for her a form of diversion. Just as I could forget my ailing father and read quietly, maybe she too could shift her mind from caregiving and think on other things.

"The truth is. . ." my mother started again.

"The truth is, I can't help thinking it would ease your father's mind if you secured a post before he passed. It looks like it may be too late, but he's still conversant and his mind is still sound. If only you could manage this one last thing for him."

I was in no position to perform such filial duty. I wrote not a word to Sensei.

Chapter 12

When my brother arrived, Father was reading the paper in bed. Father had always been an avid reader of the news, and now that he was bedridden with nothing to do, his interest was even greater. My mother and I indulged him during his illness and did not try to dissuade him.

"Great to see you're feeling so well. I'd feared for the worst, but it seems my fears were misplaced."

My brother spoke thus toward my father. To me, his tone was much too upbeat and came across as disingenuous. Away from Father's side though, when we spoke in private, he was duly subdued.

"Are you sure you should let him read the paper?"

"I'd rather he took it easy, but he insists on reading, so what can we do?"

My brother listened in silence as I explained myself.

"Does he even know what he's reading?" he asked.

He was questioning Father's mental faculty. He'd sensed, it seems, that Father's illness might have dulled his mind.

"His mind is sound. I sat with him earlier, and we spoke for a good twenty minutes on various topics. Nothing he said was off-kilter. At the rate he's going, he may hold out a while yet."

My sister's husband, who arrived around the same time as my brother, was even more sanguine. Father talked with him at length, asking after my sister.

"In her condition, I wouldn't want her hazarding a long train ride. If she overexerts herself, she'll be the one at risk," Father said.

"But don't you worry. As soon as I'm better, I'll go see the baby myself. It's time I did some traveling," he added.

When General Nogi died, Father was first to learn of it through the paper.

"It can't be! It can't be!" he exclaimed.

The rest of us, who didn't know what had happened, were surprised by his outburst.

"I was afraid for a moment he'd finally lost it," my brother told me later.

"I was caught off guard too." My sister's husband expressed a similar sentiment.

The newspaper in those days was a lifeline for us in the country. Each day we anticipated its arrival. I would sit at my father's bedside and read it through. When there wasn't time, I'd quietly carry it to my room and scan each article. The image of General Nogi in uniform, with his wife beside him in courtly dress, stuck in my mind for a long while.

The winds of sorrow carried to the farthest corners of the countryside, rustling our sleepy woods and fields. In the midst of this, a telegram from Sensei arrived unexpectedly. In a place like this, where dogs bark at a man in Western dress, the arrival of a telegram was always a big event. My mother, who had been the one to receive it, called me away from the others with an air of due gravity.

"What is it?" She waited at my side while I broke the seal.

It stated simply that Sensei wanted to see me and asked if I could come. I was unsure what this meant.

"It must be about your request for a position," my mother surmised.

I thought she might be right. At the same time, there was also something odd about it. At any rate, I was in no position, having summoned my brother and my sister's husband, to abandon my ill father and head off to Tōkyō. On consulting my mother, I wired back that I couldn't come. I added a few words to the effect that my father's illness was nearing a critical juncture. Unsatisfied to leave it at this, I followed up that same day by posting a detailed letter explaining our circumstances.

My mother, fully convinced it was about my requested position, consoled me with a disappointed look. "I'm afraid it's just come at a bad time. What can we do?"

Chapter 13

The letter I wrote was quite lengthy. Both my mother and I were confident that this time Sensei would respond. Then, two days after I'd posted my letter, another telegram arrived. All it said was that I needn't make the trip. I showed it to my mother.

"He probably intends to fill you in by letter."

To my mother, all of this confirmed that Sensei was moving on my behalf. I couldn't rule this out offhand, but it was not in fitting with Sensei as I knew him. I struggled to imagine him landing me a job.

"Anyway, he couldn't have received my letter yet, so no doubt this telegram preceded it."

I stated the obvious to my mother. After a moment of serious thought, she was compelled to voice her agreement. Whether Sensei had read my letter or not, of course, shed no light whatsoever on the current situation.

Our family doctor was coming from town that same day, and he was bringing the head doctor with him, so we talked no further on this matter. The two doctors examined their patient, flushed him out with an enema, and took their leave.

Since ordered to bedrest by his doctor, my father had relieved himself in bed and relied on others for assistance. This went against his nature, and initially he loathed the thought of it. Circumstances being what they were, though, he grudgingly acquiesced. It may have been that his illness was slowly dulling his senses, but with the passing of days he came to think nothing of such indulgence. On occasion he'd soil his futon or sheets. In contrast to the chagrin of those attending him, he himself seemed little concerned. One result of his illness was a sharp drop in the volume of his urine. This concerned his doctor. His appetite too gradually diminished. Once in a while he would get a craving, but it was only a craving of the tongue, and very little would make it past his throat. He lacked the vigor to reach for his cherished paper. The reading glasses by his pillow remained tucked away in their black sleeve. Saku, a childhood friend who still resided nearby, called to see how he was doing. Father greeted him by name and looked at him with heavy eyes.

"Saku-san, thank you for coming. I wish I had your good health. I'm afraid I'm nearing my end."

"You're doing alright. With two university graduates in the family, a little illness is nothing to complain of. Look at me. I've lost my wife and I have no children. I'm merely soldiering on. What does my health get me?"

It was several days after Saku's visit that Father was given the enema. The doctors, he said, had done a wonder on him. His mood was greatly improved, and his outlook a little less morbid. My mother, either affected by his spirits or simply hoping to encourage him further, spoke of Sensei's telegram. She talked as though a position in Tōkyō, just as he'd wished for me, had indeed been secured. I was sitting close by, beginning to feel uneasy, but I couldn't interrupt my mother. I listened in silence. Father's face was beaming.

"That's wonderful," my sister's husband added.

"Do you know what kind of work it is?" my brother asked.

By this time, I lacked the courage to challenge their misconceptions. I gave them a vague answer and rose from my seat.

Chapter 14

Father's illness brought him to death's doorstep and then appeared to hesitate. We wondered each night, as we retired, if fate's final verdict would fall the next day.

Father was not in such pain as to distress those around him. On this point, at least, caring for him was not a burden. Out of caution, one of us in turn would sit with him through the night. The rest were free to retire to their own beds at the appropriate time. On one occasion I couldn't sleep for some reason, and I thought I heard a faint groaning from the sick room. I slipped out of my own bed and went to Father's bedside to check on him. It was my mother's turn for night duty, but I found her asleep at Father's side, her head resting on her bent arm. Father was resting soundly, as though he'd been gently placed into deep slumber. I made my way quietly back to bed.

My brother and I slept under shared netting. My sister's husband, who was family but also our guest, slept alone in a separate room.

"Poor Seki. Pulled away from home and stuck here for who knows how long."

Seki was my sister's husband's family name.

"He must not be so busy, to be able to stay here with us. I'm afraid it's hardest on you if this drags on too far."

"Hardship or not, I have no choice. Other demands will have to wait."

My brother and I, with our bedding side by side, talked at night before turning in. My brother knew in his mind, and I sensed in my heart, that there was no hope for our father. We were children waiting for a parent to die. As his children, we were not inclined to speak such thoughts out loud. However, each knew full well what the other was thinking.

"Father still seems determined to recover," my brother said to me.

There was some truth to what my brother said. When the locals called to wish my father well, he always insisted on receiving them. In the course of their exchange, he never failed to bemoan the fact that he hadn't been able to fête my graduation. He sometimes added that he'd set things right as soon as he recovered.

"You're lucky your graduation party was canceled. Mine was an awful affair," my brother reminded me.

Remembering the drunken disorder of that day, I forced a smile. I could still picture the scene, with Father shamelessly pushing endless food and drink on the guests.

As brothers go, my brother and I weren't very close. We'd often quarreled growing up, and I, as the younger one, had always ended up on the losing end. Our differences in character led to divergent academic interests. During my university days, and especially after making Sensei's acquaintance, I thought of my brother from afar as much more a brute than a gentleman. I hadn't seen him in a long time, and he was living in remote quarters. Both time and space precluded any sense of connection. Even so, when we finally came together now, the natural bonds of brotherhood still held firm. The current situation accentuated these bonds and drew them tighter. At the bedside of our father, a man on the verge of death, we joined hands in common cause.

"What will you do next?" my brother asked me.

I responded with a very different question.

"How much wealth do we have?"

"I can't say. Father's never told me. Apart from property, though, I don't think there's much."

Then there was Mother, who continued to fret over Sensei's response.

"Still no letter yet?" she would press me.

Chapter 15

"Who is this man you refer to as Sensei?" my brother asked me.

"Haven't I told you already?" I replied.

Even as I asked this, I felt annoyance at my brother for disregarding all that I'd already explained.

"I know what you told me. It's just that. . ."

My brother, it turned out, was not satisfied with what he'd been told. I felt no obligation to enlighten him further. It wasn't worth the effort. Nonetheless, I was annoyed. That facet of him which chafed me so was again rearing its head.

My brother assumed that anyone I admired and addressed as Sensei must surely be a gentleman of worldly renown. At least on the order of a university professor. What merit could there be in an unknown man who'd accomplished nothing? On this point, my brother and father were of like mind. However, where my father had dismissed Sensei offhand as an impotent idler, my brother took a harsher view. Any man, he intimated, who fails to do that of which he's capable, is no man at all.

"Watch out for egoists. A life of leisure is the height of indolence. There's no excuse for squandering one's talents."

I wanted to ask my brother if he even knew what "egoist" meant.

"That being said," my brother went on, "if he can secure you a position then take it. You saw how pleased Father was."

Without confirmation from Sensei, I was disinclined to place my faith in any such outcome. At the same time, I lacked the courage to voice my doubts. Since Mother had rashly announced my triumph, I was stuck now, having no firm grounds for disavowal. With or without Mother's urging, I awaited Sensei's letter. I hoped to find in it the good news that my family was expecting. In light of my dying father, of my mother who sought so to comfort him, of my brother who disparaged men of leisure, of my aunt and uncle and others, I worried intensely now on this matter for which I'd had little regard.

Father coughed up a strange yellowish substance, and I remembered the warnings of Sensei and his wife.

"Being bedridden so long has affected his stomach," my mother concluded.

She didn't know what was happening. I looked into her eyes and was overcome with pity.

When my brother and I were together in the hearth room, he asked if I'd heard. He was referring to what the doctor had said on taking his leave. I knew full well what it was, even without having heard.

My brother turned to me. "Would you be willing to stay and take care of the house?"

I didn't answer.

"Mother can't do it alone," he added. The thought of me wasting away here, drinking in smells of the earth, seemed not to concern him. "If you just want to read your books, you can read them here in the country. You won't need to hold down a job. What could be better?"

"Isn't that the role of the eldest son?" I responded.

"You know I'm in no position to do it," he dismissed me offhand.

My brother, it seemed, was determined to make a name for himself in the world.

"If you can't do it, then we'll have to impose on our uncle. In that case, though, one of us will likely have to take Mother in."

"I'm not so sure she'll agree to leave."

Before our father was even in his grave, we were thus discussing life without him.

Chapter 16

Sometimes Father would mumble deliriously.

"General Nogi, forgive me. I've known no honor. But rest assured, I'll follow you soon."

Out of the blue he would mutter so, unsettling our mother, who would call for the family to gather at his bedside. When his mind cleared, he seemed to relish the respite from his solitude that our company offered. Whenever he didn't find Mother in the room, he would call out her name.

"Where's Omitsu?"

Even when he didn't ask for her by name, he sought her with his eyes. Many times I rose to go get her. She'd ask what he needed, stop whatever else she was doing, and come to the sickroom. Sometimes Father said nothing, but simply fixed his eyes on her. Then again, at times he would surprise her with unexpectedly tender words.

"Omitsu, to think of all you've done for me."

Mother could not help but be touched. Afterward, it seemed, she would reflect back on how Father was before, a healthy man so different from what he was now.

"He speaks so dolefully now, but that man in his day was a terror."

She would tell, for instance, of the time he took a broom and beat her over the back. This story, though my brother and I had heard it many times, was different now. Her words rang like a keepsake from our father's past.

Death's dim specter danced before Father's eyes, yet he kept his final wishes to himself.

"I wonder if we shouldn't question him while we can," my brother confided to me.

"I don't know," I answered.

I worried about the effect on him of pressing the matter from our side. Unsure what to do, the two of us consulted our uncle. Our uncle pondered the question.

"If he does have things to say, then now's the time. On the other hand, it wouldn't be right to rush him."

Father's speech finally began to falter. Then he became comatose. Mother, again not understanding, mistook this for slumber and welcomed it.

"It's easy on us all when he sleeps so soundly."

Father would sometimes open his eyes and suddenly call someone's name. The one he called for was always the one who'd been last by his side. Father was slipping in and out of consciousness. His moments of clarity, like a white thread stitching through darkness, were intermittent yet connected. It was understandable that Mother should take his comatose state for normal sleep.

As the days passed, his faculty for speech abandoned him. He would start to say something but not complete his thought, often leaving his listeners in the dark. In doing so, he would start out in a strong voice, hardly that of a man on his deathbed. For our part, we had to raise our voices and bring our mouths close to his ear.

"Would you like us to cool your head?"

"Please."

The nurse helped me to change out his water pillow and place the ice bag, loaded with fresh ice, over his head. I supported the bag lightly at the periphery of Father's hairline, giving the sharp ice shards a chance to lose their edges. In that moment, my brother came in from the hallway and quietly handed me a letter. As I received it in my open left hand, I felt there was something not right.

It was much heavier than any normal letter. It was not in a standard envelope, nor would it have fit in one. It was wrapped in writing paper, carefully glued at the seam. As my brother had handed it to me, I'd noticed it was registered mail. I flipped it over and saw Sensei's name in discreet writing on the back. Occupied as I was, I slipped it into my breast pocket. It would have to wait until later.

Chapter 17

On that day, our patient's condition seemed especially dire. When I vacated my post to go to the toilet and ran into my brother in the hallway, he asked where I was going, challenging me with the tone of a guardsman.

"His appearance concerns me. We'll need to watch him closely," he advised.

I was of the same opinion. Forgetting the letter in my pocket, I soon returned to the sickroom. Father opened his eyes and asked Mother to tell him who was present. Mother explained, one by one, who was there. Father nodded at each name. When he didn't nod, Mother repeated herself in a louder voice and confirmed with him that he'd understood.

"Thank you all for your kind care," Father said before again losing consciousness.

We watched him intently for a while. No words were spoken. Finally, one person rose and went to the next room. Then another rose. I was the third to rise, leaving for my own room. I wanted to open that letter I'd placed in my pocket. I could certainly have opened it easily enough there in the sick room. However, given its length, I couldn't well read it through on the spot. I needed to steal away and dedicate some time.

I ripped it open, tearing my way through the fibrous paper that wrapped it. What I found inside was page upon page of neatly-written characters on quad-ruled paper, much like a manuscript. The pages were bent into fourths to facilitate mailing. For ease of reading, I reversed the bends to flatten them out.

Astonished at the volume of writing, I wondered what this mass of paper and ink would tell me. At the same time, the sickroom too was weighing on my mind. If I started in reading, I was certain to be called away before finishing. I had the feeling that something would happen with Father, or if not, then that my mother or brother or uncle would need me. I couldn't settle myself to focus on Sensei's words. In a restless state I read just the opening page. Its content was as follows.

"You once asked me to tell you about my past, and at the time I lacked the courage to comply. Now, however, I believe myself at liberty to candidly tell you all. This liberty, though, is purely circumstantial, and if I await your arrival then the chance will be past. If I fail to exercise it now, the possibility of affording you the benefit of my experience will be lost forever. In such case, the promise I made that day, in full sincerity, would prove but hollow words. Having no other recourse, I set here in writing all that I should rather have told you in person."

Having read thus far, I knew now the reason for the great length of Sensei's letter. I'd doubted all along that he would trouble himself over the question of my employment. Why though would Sensei, ever the poor correspondent, take up his pen and write at such length? Why could he not wait for my return?

"He's now at liberty to tell me. This freedom, though, is fleeting and soon to be lost forever."

I repeated these words to myself, struggling to fathom their meaning. I was suddenly hit by a wave of unease. I turned to read further. In that moment, my brother called loudly from the sickroom. I rose in alarm and rushed down the hall toward the others. I steeled myself for Father's last moment, fearing it was at long last upon us.

Chapter 18

The doctor, whom I didn't realize had called, was there in the sick room. In hope of bringing comfort to his patient, he was preparing another enema. The nurse was asleep in another room, resting from the previous night's watch. My brother, unaccustomed to such tasks, was on his feet and flustered. As soon as I appeared, he instructed me to help and returned to his seat. Acting in his place, I positioned an oiled paper underneath Father's buttocks.

Father's condition eased a bit. The doctor stayed for half an hour to confirm the efficacy of the enema, then took his leave with a promise to call again soon. On his way out, he made a point to say that we should not hesitate to summon him if the situation demanded.

I withdrew from the sickroom, where a turn for the worse seemed imminent, and went back to Sensei's letter. Try as I might, though, I couldn't calm my nerves. As I sat at my desk, I imagined my brother would call at any moment. I feared that his next call would be the last, and the thought set my hands to trembling. I paged mechanically through Sensei's letter. I regarded the characters, each neatly penned within its box on the page. However, I lacked the faculty to draw out any meaning. Even skimming proved too great a chore. I flipped my way to the final page and prepared to refold the pile for safekeeping back on my desk. In that moment, one line near the end caught my eye.

"By the time this letter reaches you, I'll be gone from this world. I'll be already deceased."

I was shocked. My breast, so agitated and restless as it was, seemed to freeze in an instant. I flipped through the pages in reverse order, grabbing a line from each as I went. Eager to learn what I needed to know, I stabbed at the dancing text with my eyes. In that moment, the only question was Sensei's well-being. His past, and all the unknowns he'd promised to reveal, were no longer of consequence. As I reversed through its pages, the lengthy letter was loathe to reveal an answer. I tossed it down in frustration.

I went to the sickroom to check again on Father. To my surprise, all round the sickbed was calm. I motioned to my mother, who was seated there with a tired and helpless look, and asked how he was.

"He seems to be holding out better now," she replied.

I leaned close to Father's face. "How do you feel? Did the enema help a bit?"

Father nodded, then said, "Thank you," quite clearly. His mind was not as far gone as I'd feared.

I withdrew again from the sickroom and returned to my own room. I looked at the clock and checked the train schedule. In an instant, I was back on my feet and was straightening my sash. I dropped Sensei's letter into my sleeve pocket. After that I left through the side door. Hardly conscious of my own actions, I rushed to the doctor's house. I intended to ask him frankly if Father would last a few more days. I intended to ask his help, through injections or any means possible, to make Father hold on. Regrettably, the doctor was out. I didn't have the time, or the self-composure, to await his return. I immediately hired a rickshaw and raced to the station.

I held a piece of paper against the station wall and penciled a note to my mother and brother. It was tersely worded, but still preferable, I reckoned, to disappearing with no notice. I instructed the rickshaw driver to quickly run it back home. Then, with a burst of resolve, I jumped aboard the train bound for Tōkyō. Amid the rumbling of the third-class carriage, I pulled Sensei's letter from my sleeve pocket and read it through from start to finish.

BOOK THREE
SENSEI'S TESTAMENT

Chapter 1

. . . I received several letters from you this past summer. In the second one, if I recall correctly, you sought my assistance in securing a suitable position here in Tōkyō. My thought, when I read that, was that I ought to help. Or I felt, at least, that I should write you a proper response. However, to be perfectly honest, I made no endeavor with respect to your request. As you know, my circle of acquaintances is quite small. It might better be said, even, that I'm fully alone in this world. As such, my latitude for effectual intercession is nil. That wasn't the real problem, though. The real problem was my own struggle with the question of my existence. Whether to continue on as I am, like a mummified figure forgotten amongst the living, or whether to. . . In those days, I shuddered at the implication of the words "or whether to." Like a man who runs for a cliff edge then suddenly glimpses the bottomless depths below, I was a coward, and I agonized as all cowards do. Regrettably, I might even say that in those days I reserved no room for you in my thoughts. To state this bluntly, your lot in life and how you earned your living were of no import whatsoever. They didn't concern me in the least. I couldn't suffer such agitation. I stuck your letter in the holder, folded my arms before me, and resumed my brooding. Why should a man from a family of means, just out of school, fret about his livelihood so and kick up a fuss? I viewed you thus, from a distance, with an air of mild contempt. I divulge this by way of explanation, as I still owe you a response, and not to offend through impudence. As you read further, I believe you'll see what's truly in my heart. At any rate, I didn't write when I should have. This was wrong of me, and I wish to apologize for my negligence.

Later on I sent you a telegram. In all honestly, at that time I was wishing to see you. I was ready to share with you the story of my past, just as you'd requested. You wired back that at present you couldn't come to Tōkyō. Disappointed, I gazed for a long while at that telegram. It seemed you were not satisfied with just the telegram, and you followed up with a long letter, from which I understood fully why you couldn't come. By no means did I feel you were slighting me. How could you leave home and abandon your father on his sickbed? My request, in light of your father's condition, was inappropriate.—In truth, when I sent that telegram the plight of your father had fully slipped from my mind. That despite what I'd said to you here in Tōkyō, about the severity of his illness and how vigilant you must be in tending to him. I've exposed myself as temperamental. Maybe the weight of my past has made me so, subjugating my rational thoughts. On this point, I'm aware of my own shortcoming, and I ask for your understanding.

When I read your letter—that last one you sent—I felt as though I'd wronged you. I thought to write you back to that effect, and I took up my pen to do so, but I didn't produce a single line. If I was going to write you, it had to be this letter, which I was not yet ready to write, so I stopped. That was why I only wired back, telling you that you needn't come.

Chapter 2

Thereafter I set myself to drafting this letter. I'm unaccustomed to taking pen in hand, and it pained me greatly when events and thoughts in my head would not take shape on paper. I came close to reneging on my promise. I laid my pen down many times, but never for very long. Within the same hour I would reach for it again. I may strike you as a man consumed by adherence to obligation, and I don't deny this. As you know, I'm a solitary man with limited social contact. Turn which way I may, nowhere do I face any real obligation to speak of. By design or by nature, I've strived to live a humble and quiet life. Banishing obligation offhand, however, was never my intent. If anything, my deference toward obligation is excessive, and I lack the vigor to withstand its demands. Hence the subdued existence you've come to witness. Once I've made a promise, therefore, it troubles me deeply to renege. In your case, to avoid any such ill feeling, I found myself compelled to pick back up the pen I'd laid aside.

It's also the case that I wanted to write. Obligation aside, I want to explain my past. I believe it's fair to say that my past is my own and unique to me. It would be a shame, would it not, to depart this world without a chance to share it. This too is in part what drives me. I would never share my experiences, of course, with those not fit to receive them. Faced with such choice, I'd rather carry them to my grave. In fact, it's only you that prevents my past from remaining my own, that allows it to serve another, albeit vicariously. Of the tens of millions inhabiting Japan, it's only to you that I wish to convey my past. You're sincere. You confessed to me your sincere desire to learn of life's lessons.

I intend to unleash upon you, in full force, the darkness of humanity. You mustn't shrink from it. Study it intently, and seize from its midst that which can serve you. When I speak of darkness, I mean so in an ethical sense. I was born into and brought up in an ethical world. My concept of ethics may seem foreign to young folk today, but nevertheless, it's something thoroughly my own. By no means is it a borrowed suit, donned for expedience. For this reason, I believe that you, with a lifetime before you, can take from it something of value.

As you'll remember, you often engaged me on topics of contemporary thought, and you're well aware of how I responded. I never showed disdain for your views, but neither could I respect them. There was no substance to back them up. You were too young to draw on any real experience. I laughed at times, and received in return a dissatisfied look from you. Finally, you insisted I lay out my own past before you, unroll it like a picture scroll. In that moment, for the first time, I respected you. You showed yourself willing, in no uncertain terms, to reach within my gut and seize my very life. You were ready to cut at my heart and partake of my warm flowing blood. My life at that time was dear to me still. I felt no desire to die, so I fended you off with a promise to someday comply. I'm now prepared to rip open this heart and pour out my blood before you. It's my sincere hope that, as my own heart falls still, a new beat of life might stir within your breast.

Chapter 3

I lost both of my parents before the age of twenty. My wife, I remember, once told you of this. They both died of the same disease. As my wife mentioned, much to your surprise at the time, they died almost together, one right after the other. The truth is, my father died of abdominal typhus, a terrible disease, and my mother contracted the same while tending him.

I was their only son. We were quite well off, and I was raised in comfortable surroundings. Looking back on it all, if my parents hadn't died, or if even one had survived, I believe I would still to this day enjoy that same sense of comfort.

Their passing left me vacant and alone. I was lacking in knowledge, lacking in experience, and lacking in discernment. When my mother died, we had not even told her my father was already gone. I don't know if she sensed his passing, or whether she believed, as those around her asserted, that he was on his way toward recovery. I do know that she placed her cares in my uncle's hands. Once, when I was present with them, she gestured to me and appealed to him for my care. My parents had given me their blessing to leave for Tōkyō, and this too seemed to be on her mind. She managed the word "Tōkyō" before my uncle broke in to assure her that all would be fine. He then turned to me and praised my mother's fortitude, meaning perhaps her stamina under duress of high fever. When I think back on this now, however, I'm not fully convinced that my mother intended the words of that day as her last.

My mother, of course, knew what my father had contracted and knew of its terrible nature. She was also aware that she herself was infected. It's still not clear to me, however, that she really believed she would lose her life. The words she spoke when feverish, though coherent and concise, often vanished from her memory without so much as a trace. Accordingly. . . but I've digressed from the topic at hand. This tendency to dissect thing so, to turn them round and scrutinize every facet, was at that time already ingrained in my being. I think it's important to tell you this up front. This account, which is hardly vital to the story I intend to relate, perhaps will serve to illustrate this tendency at work. Please read it in this light. I'm disposed to viewing the conduct and actions of others through the lens of my own ethics, and over time I believe this has led me, more and more, to question people's decency.

This has certainly contributed, in no small way, to my discontent and distress. Please bear this in mind.

For the sake of coherence, I'd best set my story back on track. As I prepare to write at length, I believe myself, for a man in my situation, to be relatively well composed. The echo of the trains, that reaches one's ears when the world is sleeping, has now ceased. Outside the shutters, at some point, the insects have started their faint and doleful song, evoking thoughts of the dew-covered autumn chill. In the next room, oblivious to my endeavor, my wife is resting peacefully. The tip of my pen scratches out these characters one by one. With feeling of calm I work the page. If my pen goes astray, it's only for want of practice, not for want of a quiet mind.

Chapter 4

At any rate I was left alone, with no recourse but to heed my mother's words and rely on my uncle. My uncle, for his part, took charge and managed affairs on my behalf. Through his good graces, I was able to leave for Tōkyō as planned.

I came to Tōkyō and began my high school studies. High school students back then, in contrast to today, were a crude and rambunctious lot. One fellow I knew, in an after-hours altercation, bloodied a worker's head with his wooden clog. This was after much drink, and in the heat of trading blows he was relieved of his school cap. Inside the cap, of course, his name was neatly inscribed on a patch of white fabric. This landed him in hot water, and the police came close to taking their case to the school. Only through concerted efforts of his friends was the matter finally hushed. Your generation was raised in gentler times, and such reckless abandon probably strikes you as asinine. I can't say I disagree. At the same time, however, in students of my time was an element of authenticity that's lacking today.

The monthly allowance I received from my uncle was far less than what you receive from your father. (Though of course the cost of living was also less.) Even so, I did not feel the least bit pinched. I can also say that among my peers, when it came to money, I could hold my own and felt no need to envy others. Looking back now, I rather suspect it was I who was looked on with envy. I say this in part because, in addition to my monthly allowance, there was also book money (I was already fond of collecting books), and there were discretionary remittances I received from my uncle on request. In short, I was fairly well able to live as I pleased.

Naïve as I was, I not only trusted my uncle, but also looked up to him with a sense of gratitude. He was an entrepreneur. He was a prefectural assemblyman. I also recall his affiliation with a political party, I suppose through these same connections. He was my father's younger brother, without a doubt, but his interests in life seemed fully divergent from those of my father. My father had inherited the family wealth and was intent to a fault on preserving it. For pleasure, he indulged in the arts of tea and flowers. He was also an avid reader of poetry, and he was always quite taken with paintings and antiques. We lived in the country, but there was a town some eight kilometers distant—this was the town where my uncle resided. The curio dealer from town would sometimes call on my father with picture scrolls, incense burners, and the like. The term "man of means" seems suitable in summing up my father. He was a country gentleman of relatively refined taste.

My uncle, magnanimous by nature, was a very different man. Even so, the two of them were surprisingly close. My father saw my uncle as dependable and far more enterprising than himself. He even said once that inheriting wealth, as he had done, and not having to fend for oneself, robs a man of his edge. He said this to my mother, and he also said it to me. He intended it more for my sake, it seems, by way of guidance. "You'll do well to remember this," he added while looking directly my way. And I still do, to this day, remember it. How could I doubt this uncle whom my father so trusted and admired? This was an uncle in whom I too felt pride. My feelings toward him, when my father and mother were gone and I depended on him so, went well beyond pride. I saw him as the mainstay of my own welfare.

Chapter 5

When I first returned home for summer holiday, my uncle and his wife had taken up residence and were running the house in place of my parents. We'd agreed to this prior to my departure for Tōkyō. Given that I was alone in the world, and given that I could not stay and mind the house, this was the only workable alternative.

My uncle at that time had a hand in various ventures. In tending to his affairs, he'd pointed out by way of mild objection, his present place in town was far more convenient than my house in the country. He said this to me after the passing of my parents, when I'd consulted with him on how to manage the house during my absence in Tōkyō. My house had a long history, and it was well regarded in the region. I expect it's the same in your home town—the dismantling or sale of a pedigreed house in the country, despite their being a successor, would cause quite a stir. I'd do so now without a second thought, but I was young then and felt myself in a bind. I had to go to Tōkyō, and at the same time I had to maintain my house.

My uncle reluctantly agreed to move into the empty house. However, he insisted on keeping his place in town. For convenience in handling his affairs, he would need to commute between residences. I had, of course, no grounds for opposing this plan. Any arrangement that freed me to leave for Tōkyō was, in my mind, satisfactory.

As a young man out on my own, I still felt a strong attachment to my family home. In the spirit of a traveler, I knew there was a place I could always come home to. No matter how Tōkyō enticed me, once the holidays came, I felt a strong pull to return. I studied hard and played hard in Tōkyō, but at night I dreamt of holidays home in the country.

I didn't know of my uncle's comings and goings during my absence, but on my return his entire family was gathered under my roof. I expect that his school-aged children spent most of their time in town, but they were on holiday too now and enjoying time in the country.

All were happy to see me. I was glad to see the house so full of activity, much livelier now than in my parents' days. My uncle displaced his eldest son, who had taken over my room, and put him elsewhere. There were plenty of rooms, so I offered to lodge in another, but my uncle wouldn't hear of it, reminding me that it was my house.

Other than an occasional reflection on my parents, I passed a carefree summer with my uncle's family and returned to Tōkyō. However, there was one thing that summer that cast a slight pall over my stay. Both my uncle and his wife, despite the fact that I'd just started high school, advised that I marry. They brought this up repeatedly. The first time, it was completely out of the blue and caught me off guard. The second time, I clearly declined. The third time, I was compelled to ask why they persisted. Their thought process was simple. I should take a bride and return home to assume my father's place as master of the house. In my mind, coming home for holidays was enough. On the other hand, what they said was not unreasonable. My father's place was mine to take, and to do so I'd need a bride. Versed as I was in the ways of the country, I could understand this. I don't believe I was dead set against it. However, I'd just begun my studies in Tōkyō, and such notions seemed far away, as though viewed via scope from a remote vantage. I left home again, with my uncle's wish unanswered.

Chapter 6

I thought no more on the matter of marriage. In the faces of the young men around me was no trace of marital or domestic concern. All were free, and all, it seemed, were masters of their own destinies. Amongst these carefree souls, if one dug deeply, there were perhaps some who, compelled by family circumstances, had already taken a wife. However, I was too naïve understand this at the time. Those in such situations likely refrained from disclosing their private affairs, out of deference toward fellow students for whom such thoughts were still so distant. It occurred to me later that I myself was in fact in such a circumstance. Without yet knowing this, though, I pursued my studies with carefree innocence.

At the end of the school year, I packed up my things and returned to the country and the place of my parents' graves. Just as the year before, I found the familiar faces of my uncle and his children in the house of my parents. I drank in again the smells of home. Such smells were still dear to me. In part, I believe, for the welcome respite they offered from the routine of the school year.

In the midst of these smells of my childhood, however, I was accosted again by my uncle on the matter of marriage. His persuasions were simply those of the year prior, restated. His arguments were the same, but this time, unlike the year prior, he had a specific match in mind. This put me in an uncomfortable position. The match was none other than his own daughter, who would of course be my cousin. According to my uncle, taking her as my bride would be advantageous to both families, and my father, in the past, had been of like mind. I could see the advantage in this. I could also imagine that my father and uncle might have discussed it. However, until my uncle broached it, the thought had never crossed my mind.

At any rate, I was caught off guard. I was caught off guard, but I also saw the sense in what my uncle proposed. Perhaps I'd been oblivious to the world around me. If that were the case, then indifference toward this cousin was by and large the cause. From my childhood, I'd frequented my uncle's house in town. I'd sometimes spent the night there. This cousin and I had grown very close. As I'm sure you're aware, romantic feelings do not arise among siblings. It may be that I'm extending this principle to my own ends, but I believe that the same applied to this cousin and me. Having spent so much time together, and having become so familiar with each other, there was no hope for the fresh sensations of romance. Just as the first whiff of incense or the first taste of saké most excites the senses, there seems to exist, in the flow of time, a critical juncture for the stirring of romance. Once having passed it unawares, familiarity only grows with each interaction, and by and by, receptivity to romance is lost. Try as I might, I could not imagine this cousin as my wife.

My uncle was willing, if I insisted, to wait on my graduation. At the same time, he encouraged me to "strike while the iron is hot" and marry without delay. Neither option appealed to me, as I took no interest in the intended bride. I turned him down. My uncle scowled at me. My cousin cried. She was not upset that we weren't to be wed. Being rejected as a bride had simply damaged her female pride. I knew full well that she felt no more attraction for me than I for her. I departed again for Tōkyō.

Chapter 7

My third return home was a year hence, at the start of the next summer. As soon as year-end exams were over, I immediately bolted Tōkyō. Such was the pull of my native place. You've probably felt this too. The air of one's birthplace is different, and the scents of its soil are special. Fond memories of one's parents permeate the place. To spend two months of the year, July and August, lying still in the midst of this, like a snake warm in its den, was for me the best feeling imaginable.

In my simple mind, there was no need for further worry over my cousin and the question of our marriage. If one doesn't agree to something, one turns it down, and the matter is thereupon settled. This was how I saw things. The fact that I'd defied my uncle's wishes, therefore, did not concern me. I'd hardly thought of it over the intervening year, and I rushed home with my usual enthusiasm.

On returning, however, I found my uncle a different man. He didn't seem happy to see me, and he didn't welcome me as before. I'd been raised in a household loosely bound to protocol, so it was only after four or five days that this fully sank in. Some occurrence triggered something, and I suddenly felt myself ill at ease. What struck me as strange was not just my uncle. It was my aunt too. And my cousin. Even my uncle's eldest son, who had just finished middle school and had written me to inquire about vocational schools in Tōkyō, seemed strange.

By my very nature, I couldn't help but dwell on this. Why did things feel so different? Or rather, why had these others changed so? My deceased parents, I suspected, had intervened to open my half-closed eyes, and suddenly I was seeing the world for what it was. Somewhere deep down I believed that my parents, while no longer of this world, continued to love me no less than before. I had at the time, of course, no deficiencies in faculty of reason. At the same time, though, the superstitions of my ancestors coursed within me and worked their will. They're in me still to this day.

I went alone to the hillside and knelt before my parents' graves. My feeling as I knelt there was half of sorrow and half of gratitude. I felt that the two of them, reposing now beneath the cold stone, still held my future in their hands. I prayed for their care in watching over my fate. You may laugh this off as nonsense, and I suppose it's fine if you do. However, this is the person that I was.

My world had turned upside down. This wasn't for me the first such experience. I remember my great astonishment at sixteen or seventeen, when it suddenly hit me that the world was full of beauty. I couldn't believe my eyes. I rubbed them again and again. My heart cried out in exaltation. The age of sixteen or seventeen of course, in a young man or young woman, is a time of sensual awakening. For the first time, I was awake to a new beauty in the world, embodied in the female form. With regard to the opposite sex, whose existence I'd hardly noticed, the scales had fallen and my eyes were suddenly open. From that point on, heaven and earth were utterly new to me.

When I first saw my uncle for what he was, it was the same sort of awakening. All was suddenly clear. I was granted no premonition, nor chance for preparation. It was on me out of the blue. In an instant, I saw my uncle and his family in an entirely different light. I was astonished. Remaining in their care, I feared, could only lead to bad ends.

Chapter 8

Up to this point, I'd entrusted the family's assets to my uncle, but I felt now that I owed it to my parents to make myself smarter. My uncle was a self-professed "busy man," always hurrying place to place. He came and went between the house and his lodgings in town, two days here, then three days there. Thus he moved about, day after day, always looking flustered. He never failed to mention, too, how busy he was. Before I'd come to distrust him, I'd presumed he was, in fact, busy. Or at least, in my cynical moments, I'd assumed his busy airs a necessary part of his modern persona. However, now that I required his time to review the family assets, I began to perceive his busyness as nothing more than a pretext for avoiding me. It was no easy task to get time with him.

I heard that my uncle had a mistress in town. I heard this from a friend, a former middle school classmate. I wouldn't put it past this uncle to have a mistress, but I'd never heard such rumors while my father lived, and I was duly taken aback. There were various other things that I also heard from this friend. One was that my uncle's businesses had flirted with insolvency. Then, over the past several years, the situation had suddenly reversed itself. This seemed to confirm my misgivings.

I finally brought my uncle to the bargaining table. "Bargaining table" may not be quite the right word, but given how things played out in the natural course of events, I can think of no better way to describe it. My uncle was intent on treating me as a child. I confronted him, from the start, with an air of suspicion. There was no hope for any amicable resolution.

Regrettably, I can't detail here the particulars of all that transpired. There's too much else to tell. There are things of far greater import still to be written. It's only with difficulty that I restrain my pen and keep it from racing ahead. The chance to see you and relate all in due time is lost to me now. Because I'm unpracticed with the pen, and because the time left me is precious, I'm forced to refrain from telling all I would like.

You'll remember, I trust, the time I told you there are no archetypal villains in this world. How I told you that villains, in their time, emerge from the ranks of the virtuous. How one can never be too cautious. You pointed out to me, on that occasion, that I was worked up. You then asked what it is that changes a virtuous man to a villain. When I simply replied "money," you seemed disappointed. I remember well that look on your face. I can tell you now that in that moment I was thinking of my uncle. I was thinking of him with contempt. He was proof to me that money can turn any man to a scoundrel. He was proof to me that no man can be trusted. You were ready for deeper ideas, and no doubt regarded my answer as trite and unsatisfying. My answer, though, was genuine. You remember, don't you, how worked up I'd become. I believe that a straightforward reply, stated with passion on one's tongue, is more impactful than novel words from a cool head. It's the flow of blood that powers the body. Words are more than waves disturbing the air, they induce great action in broader realms.

Chapter 9

To state it bluntly, my uncle cheated me of my wealth. It was easily done in my absence, in the three years I spent in Tōkyō. From a worldly perspective, I'd proven myself a bona fide fool, happily entrusting my uncle with all matters. From a higher perspective, however, I could perhaps be seen as a noble young man, pure of heart. Looking back on my younger self, I greatly regret my innocence. If only I'd been born more tainted. At the same time, though, I somehow wish I could go back and live again as I once was. Please bear in mind that you knew me only after I'd been sullied. If "superior" refers to one defiled with the passing of years, then you can regard me as your superior.

In material terms, would I have done better in marrying my uncle's daughter as he'd proposed? I don't believe that's the case. Pushing his daughter on me had simply been part of his scheme. Far from a good-faith effort on behalf of both families, he'd been motivated all along, in proposing that I marry, by his own devious interests. I'd felt no love toward my cousin, but neither had I felt any particular dislike. Looking back on it now though, I find some comfort in the fact that I defied my uncle. Marriage or not, he'd have cheated me either way. In refusing to marry my cousin, I at least was cheated on my own terms and not on his. This is splitting hairs, though, and hardly relevant. From your vantage it must, I imagine, seem like some foolish fixation.

Other relatives intervened. I didn't trust these other relatives either. Not only did I not trust them, I viewed them as adversaries. Once aware of my uncle's treachery, I was convinced that these others were treacherous as well. If true of my uncle, whom my father had held in such high regard, then much more so of these others. Such was my logic.

They did, on my behalf, pull together all that was duly mine. When everything was appraised, it was far less than I'd expected. I could accept it without objection, or I could challenge my uncle publicly in court. These were my two options. I was indignant. I was lost as to what I should do. Litigation, I feared, would prove a lengthy process. I was in the middle of my studies, and I hated the thought of losing precious time. After much consideration, I asked my old middle school friend, who lived in town, to liquidate everything for me. My friend advised against this, but I didn't listen. I'd already decided I was leaving and not coming back. I swore to myself I would never again see my uncle's face.

Before departing, I went once more to the graves of my father and mother. I haven't seen these graves since.

Nor will I ever see them again.

My friend handled things according to my wishes. This all happened, though, a good while after my arrival in Tōkyō. Selling farmland and such in the countryside is no easy task. Prospective buyers are apt to take advantage of the situation. In the end, the amount I received was significantly less than market value. In all honesty, my assets were nothing more than some public bonds I'd left home with and the later remittance from my friend. My parents' bequest, without a doubt, had been greatly diminished. The fact that this was in no way my own doing made it all the much harder to swallow. At the same time, I had more than enough to sustain my studies. In truth, I didn't spend but half of my interest income. This abundance during my student days, as it turned out, would have wholly unforeseen consequences.

Chapter 10

With ample funds at my disposal, I thought to quit my boisterous lodgings and set up a home for myself. However, for numerous reasons this was easier said than done. I'd have to procure household wares, and I'd need to bring on an old woman as caretaker. I'd have to be sure that my old woman was trustworthy, that I could go away and leave the house in her care without worry. One day I set out for a walk and, somewhat whimsically, decided to hunt for a house as I went. From Hongōdai I descended to the west, then climbed the hill from Koishikawa toward Denzūin Temple. The area has changed completely since the rail line came through, but back then there was just the earthen wall of the artillery arsenal on the left and empty, uncultivated grassland on the right. I stood in the grass and let my mind wander as I surveyed the opposing bluffs. It's a nice view even today, but the appearance of that west side was quite different then. There was thickly grown verdure as far as the eye could see, and its effect was soothing. I wondered if I might not find some suitable place thereabouts. Without hesitation, I waded through the grass and then headed north up a narrow lane. The area, even today, is still not a proper town. Its houses are ramshackle, and back then they were even more so. I walked the neighborhood, through alleyways and side streets. Finally, I ducked into a corner sweets shop and asked the proprietress if there wasn't some modest house for rent. She inclined her head in thought for a moment, then indicated that nothing came to mind. Accepting that there were no immediate prospects, I made to leave. As I did so, she asked if I would be interested in a boarding house. My thinking changed a bit. I began to see the advantage to this. As a solitary lodger in a quiet boarding house, I'd be spared the troubles of running my own place. I took a seat in the shop and asked the proprietress for details.

It was the family of a military man, or rather the surviving family members, who lived in the house. The husband, the proprietress told me, was said to have perished in the time of the Sino-Japanese War. Up until the prior year, the family had remained near the military academy in Ichigaya. The grounds were too large, though, with a stable and such, so they'd sold the place and moved. However, they now found their new surroundings lonesome, so they'd put out a request for introduction of a suitable lodger. I learned from the proprietress that there were only the widow, her daughter, and a maidservant residing there. I thought to myself that this could be ideal—a quiet setting. I was also concerned, though, that if one like myself suddenly appeared on their doorstep, they'd regard me as just some unknown student and reject me outright. I thought about giving it up. On the other hand, for a student my appearance was hardly shabby, and I was sporting my university cap. You may find it amusing, the idea that this cap would mean anything. Unlike the present, however, university students in those days were greatly respected. In this situation, I drew confidence from my four-cornered cap. Following the instructions of the sweets shop proprietress, I called on the family cold, with no introduction.

I met the widow and explained my reason for coming. She questioned me about my background, the school, my area of study. Seemingly satisfied with the exchange, she responded on the spot that I was welcome to move in at any time. The widow was a proper woman, candid in her manner. If all military wives were like this, then I counted myself impressed. I was impressed, but also surprised. Nowhere in her temperament, I thought, was there any suggestion of loneliness.

Chapter 11

I moved in right away. I rented the room that the widow and I had talked about during my initial visit. It was the best room in the house. This was at a time when they were building upscale boarding houses in the Hongō area, so I was familiar with the finest of rooms that could be had by a student. This room I now presided over was better by far. For a while after moving, I thought it too much for a student such as myself.

It was an eight-mat room. Next to the alcove was a rack of staggered shelves, and opposite the veranda was a large closet. There were no windows, but the veranda was south-facing and received ample sun.

On my move-in day, I found in the alcove an arrangement of flowers with a koto propped next to them. Neither of these were to my liking. Having grown up with a father who fancied poetry, calligraphy, and the art of tea, my tastes from a young age were tuned to Chinese tradition. Likely due to this same influence, I'd grown to disdain frivolous adornments.

My father's curios collection had largely been laid to waste by my uncle. However, some small number of articles remained. Before leaving home, I'd had my old middle school friend take them into his charge. From the collection, I'd then chosen the several scrolls that I liked best and brought them with me, packing them loosely in the bottom of my baggage. As soon as I moved in, I'd planned to hang these in the alcove where I could appreciate them. On seeing the flowers and koto, though, my resolve failed me. When I later learned that the flowers had been placed there on my behalf, I smiled a bitter smile to myself. The koto had always been kept there. There was no other place for it, so there it had to remain.

As you read this, no doubt the notion of a young lady will be playing in your mind. My curiosity on this matter, even before I'd moved in, had already been aroused. Perhaps the anticipation of her had worked to unsettle me, or perhaps it was a general discomfort with strangers, but my greeting on our initial encounter was far from composed. The young lady too, for her part, blushed.

Based on the widow's appearance and manner, I'd constructed an image in my mind of her daughter. The image I'd constructed, however, was none too flattering. I'd built it sequentially—the wife of a military man was such, and the daughter of the wife of a military man was so. With one glance at the young lady's countenance, my exercise in conjecture was thoroughly put to shame. My mind was infused with a new and heretofore unimagined admiration for the opposite sex. From that moment, the flowers in the alcove ceased to offend me. The koto stored alongside them, likewise, was no longer intrusive.

Those flowers, when their time had passed, were regularly refreshed. The koto too was often carried off to another room, around the corner and diagonally opposite mine. I would sit at my desk, chin propped in my hands, and listen to its sound. I couldn't judge whether it was played well or not. Based on the simplicity of technique, however, I had to believe it was nothing masterful. I had to conclude it was no better than the flowers. I do know something about flowers, and the young lady's arrangements were certainly nothing worth noting.

Be that as it may, a succession of flowers unapologetically adorned my alcove. The arrangements, of course, were always in the same style. The vase, too, was always the same. Of the flowers and music, though, the music was far more eccentric. All one could hear were twangs of the strings. The vocals were absent. It wasn't that she didn't sing, but she sang in a soft voice, almost a whisper. When reproved in her playing, her voice would fade entirely.

I took pleasure in the sight of these uninspired flowers, and I took pleasure in the sound of this unpracticed koto.

Chapter 12

By the time I'd left my hometown, my outlook on life had grown quite dark. The conviction that others cannot be trusted, it seemed, had firmly taken root in my bones. I'd come to regard my uncle and aunt and other relatives, who in my mind were adversaries, as proxies for all mankind. Even on the train, I'd found myself unwittingly scrutinizing my fellow passengers. Any who ventured to engage me merely stoked my suspicions. My soul was beaten down. It often felt heavy, as though I'd swallowed lead. At the same time, as I've just described, my nerves were keenly on edge.

I think this is largely what drove me to quit my lodgings after returning to Tōkyō. I can make the case that financial freedom spurred me to set off on my own, but my former self, even with the means to do so, would never have gone to such lengths.

Even after relocating to Koishikawa, this tension within me persisted. I felt shame at the way I nervously surveyed my surroundings. Curiously enough, only my mind and my eyes functioned keenly. My mouth, in contrast, grew less and less active. Sitting silently at my desk, I observed the others in cat-like fashion. I sometimes felt bad for them, subjected to my constant mistrust. I felt like a thief in their midst, albeit one who refrains from theft. At times I fell to self-loathing.

This must strike you as odd. How could I, in such a state, feel affection toward the young lady? How could I gaze happily at her uninspired flowers? In the same vein, how could I listen with pleasure to her unpracticed koto? All I can say in response to such questions is that the feelings I've described to you were genuine. You can work out the explanation in your own mind, but I will add here just one more thought. My trust in humanity was gone with regard to money, but not with regard to love. This may come across as strange, and I too was aware of the inconsistency, but in my heart these feelings coexisted nonetheless.

I came to address the widow as Okusan, so from here on I'll refer to her thus. Okusan regarded me as quiet and mild-mannered. She also praised the diligence with which I applied myself to my studies. All the same while, she never once mentioned my anxious eyes or shiftiness of manner. I don't know if this was restraint or simply failure to take notice, but at any rate it seemed not to concern her. Not only that, but on one occasion, with a hint of admiration in her voice, she even declared me largehearted. Honest as I am, I blushed a bit and refuted her words. She proceeded to explain, in all seriousness, how I was unaware of my own virtues. Initially she had not intended to take in a student such as myself. When she'd asked the neighbors for an introduction, her intention had been to let out a room to a worker from a government office or some such place. The image she'd held in her mind was a man of limited means, a man with no other option but to dwell as a boarder. When she praised me as largehearted, she was comparing me to this boarder of her own imagining. Compared to this man living hand to mouth, at least where money was concerned, I may have been largehearted. Money and temperament, however, are two different things, the one having no connection to the other. Okusan, as women are wont to do, was intent on extending a single notion to apply to my entirety.

Chapter 13

Okusan's manner, in due course, began to work on my mood. After a time, my eyes relaxed themselves and were less shifty. My mind, I began to feel, was again rooted in the present. In short, by paying no heed to my jaundiced eyes and mistrustful demeanor, Okusan and the rest of the household did great wonders for my well-being. My nerves, with no feedback to vindicate their misgivings, gradually calmed.

Okusan was a woman of understanding, and it's possible that she consciously treated me as she sensed I needed to be treated. Then again, it's also possible that she really did regard me as largehearted, just as she professed. My anxiety was a phenomenon of my mind, and it's conceivable that its outward expression was muted. Perhaps Okusan failed to see it.

As my spirit calmed, I grew close to the family. I came to converse with Okusan and her daughter. Some days, they would call me to their room for tea. On other evenings, I would bring home sweets and invite the two of them to join me. I felt my sphere of social intercourse had suddenly expanded. To this end, precious time for study was whiled away. Curiously, though, I didn't rue the intrusion in the least. Okusan was a woman of leisure. Her daughter, however, had flower and koto classes on top of her schoolwork and should have been pressed for time, yet somehow never seemed hurried. The three of us, whenever the situation allowed, would gather together and enjoy each other's company.

It was usually the daughter who came to call me. Sometimes she would follow the veranda around the corner and stop in front of my room, and sometimes she would cut through the hearth room and appear at the fusuma that opened to the adjoining room. She would pause for a moment, then call my name and ask if I was studying. I usually had my eyes on some difficult text that lay open before me on my desk, giving the appearance of industrious study. Truth be told, however, I wasn't engaged so earnestly in my texts. My eyes would be on the page, but my thoughts were in waiting for her to come call me. When she didn't come, I felt compelled to get up myself. I would stop outside the other room and call in the same way, asking if she was studying.

The daughter had a six-mat room adjacent to the hearth room. Okusan was sometimes in the hearth room and sometimes with her daughter. In short, while the rooms were distinctly partitioned, mother and daughter occupied both, moving freely between them as though they were one and the same. When I called from without, it was always Okusan who invited me in. Even when present, the daughter seldom replied.

Over time there came to be occasions when the daughter would come to my room alone on some errand and stay to talk. On those occasions, I found myself ill at ease. I could not, I decided, attribute my unease solely to the presence of a young lady. I'd begin to fidget. I'd imagine my manner was strained, and I'd fear it might betray me. The other party, however, seemed utterly unconcerned. Seeing her so carefree, it was hard to believe she was the same girl who sang so softly with her koto. If she stayed too long, her mother would call to her from the hearth room. Sometimes she would answer back but still remain fixed where she was. Even at this, she was anything but childish. This was quite clear to me. It was also clear that she wanted me to know this.

Chapter 14

Once the young lady was gone, I would finally relax. At the same time, I would rue her absence profoundly.

Perhaps I was effeminate in my manner. To a modern young man like yourself, it must certainly seem so.

However, I was typical of those of my time.

Okusan rarely left the house. On occasions when she did leave, she never left me alone with her daughter. I can't say whether this was by chance or design. It may be pretentious to say so, but it appeared to me, based on my observations, that she was working to bring her daughter and me closer. At the same time, there were certain occasions when she seemed to have her guard up against me. When I first caught on to this, I struggled with how to react.

I wished for Okusan to make her intentions clear. Her thoughts and actions were clearly inconsistent. With my uncle's deception still fresh in my mind, though, I couldn't help harboring deeper doubts. One aspect of her behavior, I decided, must be genuine, and the other must then be a ruse. That was as far as my reasoning took me. I could draw no further conclusion, nor could I offer up any rational explanation for her behavior. Failing to unearth any pretext, all I could do was attribute it all to feminine flaws. That's just the way women are. Women, after all, are foolish things. Whenever reason failed me, this was where my thoughts invariably landed.

My disparagement of women did not extend to the young lady. In her presence, my theorizing fell flat and ceased to serve me. The affection I felt toward her bordered on faith. It may seem strange to you that I should apply this word, borrowed from the realm of religion, to a young lady, but even today I still feel this way. I'm firmly convinced that true love and religious devotion are kindred spirits. Every time I set eyes on this young lady's face, I felt myself cleansed. Every time I thought of her, a rush of noble feeling washed through me. If this wondrous thing we call love has two sides, with spiritual connections on the high side and carnal desires on the low side, then my affections were surely anchored to its uppermost point. I was, of course, a human being embodied in the flesh. However, in the eyes that regarded this young lady, and in the soul that yearned for her, thoughts of the flesh were none to be found.

Even as I harbored animosity toward the mother, my affections for the daughter grew deeper. Compared to my early days as a lodger, the relationship between the three of us was becoming complex. This complexity was of course internal and didn't show on the surface. At some point, however, I began to wonder if I hadn't misjudged the mother. I began to see that maybe there was no falsehood in her conflicting views of me. Furthermore, I began to think that these conflicting views did not rule her spirit in turn, but rather that both coexisted at all times within her breast. It seemed contradictory that Okusan would strive to bring me close to her daughter while putting up defenses against me. Then again, even when her defenses were up, I could see that she still sought to draw us closer. I believe she was simply averse to the idea of the two of us becoming overly intimate. As I had no intention of accosting the daughter in any carnal fashion, I thought her concerns unwarranted. At the same time, though, I was able put my ill will toward her to rest.

Chapter 15

Regarding all facets of Okusan's behavior as a whole, I finally concluded that within her household I was duly trusted. I even had reason to believe that I'd been deemed trustworthy from our initial encounter. To one like me, who harbored a general mistrust in his bosom, this revelation was quite surprising. I decided that women, in comparison to men, must be that much more intuitive. At the same time, I wondered if that wasn't how men managed to deceive them. In retrospect, it's funny that I could regard Okusan so while blindly trusting my own intuition with respect to her daughter. While pledging in my heart to trust no one, I trusted Okusan's daughter absolutely, all the while wondering at Okusan's trust in me.

I didn't talk much of home. I said nothing at all of what had transpired there. It pained me even to think of it. As much as I could, I let them talk while I listened. However, I couldn't keep this up. They wanted to know about my home and what it was like. I finally told them all. That I was never going back. That there was nothing there for me now, nothing save the graves of my parents. When I told them all this, Okusan was visibly moved. Her daughter wept. I decided I'd done right in divulging my past. I was glad to have done so.

After hearing my story, Okusan's expression all but told me that I'd validated her intuition. From that point on, she treated me no differently than she would her own younger kinfolk. I took no offense at this, and in fact it rather pleased me. The mistrust in my heart, however, was before long rekindled.

My doubts about Okusan began with the smallest of things. The smallest of things, however, as they recur over time, can give rise to serious doubts. Somewhere along the way, I began to wonder if Okusan wasn't pushing her daughter on me, just as my uncle had done. This woman, whom I'd thought a person of kindness, all of a sudden appeared to me a cunning schemer. Contempt welled from within me.

Okusan had made it known from the start that her house was too quiet and she wished, therefore, to take in a boarder. I didn't doubt this. After we grew close and I'd learned more about her, this motive still seemed valid. On the other hand, her financial situation was far from secure. In the interest of her own material comfort, I was not an unattractive prospect.

Once again I put up my guard. Being on guard against the mother, however, was of little avail, as my affections toward the daughter continued unattenuated. Inwardly, I derided myself. I cursed my own foolishness. This conflict in my heart, though, however foolish, was nothing to caused me pain. It was doubts of the daughter, that she might be as much the schemer as her mother, that first brought on my anguish. The thought that the two of them, behind my back, were scheming this all, was at once unbearable. I wasn't merely displeased. I was utterly and hopelessly despondent. Even at that, there was a part of me that firmly believed in the daughter. I was caught halfway between devotion and distrust, frozen in place. Both were unreal, and at the same time both were the truth.

Chapter 16

I attended my classes as usual. However, the voices of the lecturers, standing on the dais, seemed to echo from far away. The same went for my studies. I took in words with my eyes, but they vanished like smoke before they could settle in my mind. I also grew reticent. Several friends misunderstood this. They assumed I was indulging in contemplations, and even conveyed this to others. I didn't try to disabuse them, but rather was grateful for the convenient façade. There were times, though, when I was not content to let this stand and would deliberately confound them with bouts of fitful revelry.

Guests were rare in the house where I lodged. The family seemed to have few relations. Sometimes the daughter would have a friend from school over, but they would always talk so quietly that one hardly knew they were there. It didn't occur to me, of course, that their discretion might be out of deference. Those who called on me were hardly unruly, but neither did they show particular deference to others in the house. In this sense, I was a lodger living as though I owned the place, while the young lady of the house behaved like a humble guest.

I write this because it comes to mind, but it's really of no consequence. There is one thing, however, that is of consequence. I suddenly discerned one day, from the hearth room or the young lady's room, the sound of a male voice. Unlike my own visitors, this voice was exceedingly soft. I couldn't make out what was said. Not knowing what they were up to put my nerves on edge. I sat there strangely agitated. I wondered if it was a relative, or perhaps just some acquaintance.

Next I considered whether it might be a young man or someone older. Sitting where I was, I had no way of knowing. At the same time, I couldn't very well get up, walk over, and open the shōji for a look. My nerves were more than agitated. They knocked me about from inside. After the guest had departed, I made certain to ask who it was. Neither Okusan nor the daughter gave anything more than the briefest of answers. While my dissatisfaction was plain for all to see, I lacked the audacity to probe further. They were under no obligation, of course, to inform me. I maintained my self-respect, a self-respect instilled by an upbringing that emphasized dignity. At the same time, I wore with abandon a wistful look on my face. They both laughed. It may have been good-natured and fully free of derision. Then again, it may have been just the guise of good nature. I'd so lost my composure that, in the moment, all was unclear. Even after the fact, I couldn't make up my mind as to whether I'd been ridiculed.

I was a free man. I could quit my studies at any time, go and live wherever I pleased, or marry whomever I liked. There was no one whose blessing I needed. More than once, I'd resolved to approach Okusan and ask for her daughter's hand. Each time, however, I'd wavered and held back my words. It wasn't for fear of rejection. I didn't know how rejection might alter my fate, but I imagined it would simply set me on a new course, with the fresh wide world once again open before me. This was nothing I couldn't face. The one thing I couldn't face, though, was entrapment. Nothing was more mortifying than the thought of being manipulated. After my uncle had deceived me, I'd sworn that, come what may, I'd never be taken again.

Chapter 17

Seeing me buy only books, Okusan suggested I should have some clothes made as well. All I owned, in fact, were my country-woven cottons. Students in those days did not wear silk. A friend of mine was from a family of merchants or whatnot in Yokohama who lived the lavish life. On one occasion, he received a fine silk vest by courier. We all made sport at the sight of it. He became self-conscious and tried to defend it, but in the end he tossed this vest, procured at some expense, into the bottom of his trunk. A bunch of us then pressured him into putting it on. Unfortunately, as it turned out, the vest had attracted lice. My friend, playing this in his own favor, wadded up the offending article and tossed it into a large ditch in Nezu while out walking. I was with him on his walk and watched this all from the top of the bridge with amusement. Nowhere within me was the least tinge of regret at the wastefulness of his act.

I'd matured a good deal since that time. However, I was still not so discerning as to feel the need for visiting attire. Until much later, when I'd finished my studies and was sporting a mustache, I retained the eccentric view that clothes weren't worth my worry. I replied to Okusan that books were a necessity and clothing was not. Okusan knew how many books I was buying. She asked if I'd read them all. Among my purchases were dictionaries, and there were also some books that I'd intended to look at but whose pages had never been cracked. I struggled for an answer. It occurred to me then that since I was buying things I didn't need, clothes were no worse than books. I also wanted, on the pretext of return for kindness received, to buy the daughter something nice—an obi or a length of fabric that would be to her liking. I entrusted all this to Okusan.

Okusan did not propose to go alone. She insisted that I come with. She also wanted her daughter along. To those like myself, brought up in earlier times, it was not a student's place to walk in public in the company of a young lady. I was much more a slave to custom then than I am now, and I wavered a bit before mustering the courage to acquiesce.

The daughter was dressed in her best. She'd applied a generous layer of powder over her already fair skin, making her quite the sight. She caught the eye of all who passed us by. After looking at her, they would next direct their gaze toward me. I found it disquieting.

The three of us bought what we needed at Nihonbashi. It took longer than expected, as we were slow to decide. Okusan would call out my name and ask my opinion of things. Sometimes she would drape fabric down from her daughter's shoulders and ask me to step back and look. I would signal my approval or distaste. To my credit, I always managed some decent manner of reply.

We took our time in this way, and it was already dinnertime when we left for home. Okusan offered to treat me somewhere, and she led us into a narrow lane. There was a theater there called Kiharadana. The lane was narrow, and its eating establishments were likewise confined. The area was completely unfamiliar to me, and I was impressed how Okusan knew where to go.

We returned home late in the evening. The next day was Sunday, and I spent the day holed up in my room. On Monday morning I went to class and was chided first thing by a classmate. He made a point of asking when I'd taken a wife. He then went on to praise her as a rare beauty. He'd seen the three of us, no doubt, during our outing in Nihonbashi.

Chapter 18

When I returned home, I shared this with Okusan and her daughter. Okusan laughed. Then, however, she looked at me and asked if I hadn't been annoyed. This, I thought to myself at the time, is how women sound out men for their feelings. Okusan's eyes held a look that confirmed as much. I perhaps should have told her candidly, then and there, exactly what my feelings were. Within me was a lingering lump of suspicion, though, that held me in check. I started to speak and then stopped myself. I proceeded instead to deflect the conversation onto a tangent.

I extracted my all-important self from the picture, probing for Okusan's thoughts on her daughter's marriage. Okusan did not hide the fact that there'd been several suitors. She explained, though, that she felt no need to rush things. After all, her daughter was still young and still in school. While she never stated it, she seemed to place great faith in her daughter's beauty. When the time came, she told me, she could certainly find a match. At the same time, she only had one child, and she was loathe to give her away. She seemed undecided between marrying off her daughter or taking in a son-in-law.

I felt I'd learned much from this exchange. In doing so, however, I'd effectively squandered an opportunity. I couldn't slip in a single word now on my own behalf. I sought a suitable stopping point to break off and retire to my room.

The daughter, who'd been nearby and laughed off my friend's comments as nonsense, had at some point removed herself to the far corner and was sitting with her back to me. I saw her there as I turned my head in rising to leave. From the backside, a person's heart is opaque. I had no idea what her thoughts might be. She was sitting before the closet. Its door was open a bit, and she seemed to be looking at something that she had taken out and placed on her lap. Through the gap in the door, my eye caught a glimpse of the fabrics we'd purchased two days prior. Mine and hers were stacked together in the same corner.

As I silently rose from my seat, Okusan suddenly asked in a serious tone what I thought. Her manner was so abrupt that I had to ask in return what she meant. After she clarified that the question concerned her daughter, and whether she should marry her off sooner versus later, I replied that I thought she should take her time. She confirmed that she, too, was of the same mind.

At this point in my relationship with Okusan and her daughter, another young man, by necessity, entered the picture. His inclusion in the household would alter my fate most profoundly. Had his path not intersected with mine, it is unlikely I would be writing you, as I now am, to leave behind this lengthy account. You could say, in a sense, that the devil passed before me, casting a shadow on the whole of my existence, as I stood there unawares. I should confess that it was I who brought this young man into the house. I did so, of course, with Okusan's consent. Initially, even after I explained everything to her in broaching the idea, she opposed me. I had ample reason for bringing this young man in, while Okusan had no sound argument in support of her opposition. In the end, I prevailed. I pressed my case with resolve, and proceeded as I thought best.

Chapter 19

I'll refer to that friend here as K. K and I were close from childhood. Being close from childhood, it goes without saying that we share the same hometown roots. K was the son of a Shinshū priest. He was not the eldest son, though, but the second. That being the case, he was sent to the house of a certain physician as an adopted son. The Honganji sect held great influence in my home region, and a Shinshū priest could live in relative comfort. As an example, if a priest had a daughter, and that daughter came of marriageable age, the parishioners would band together and find a suitable household into which she could marry. The expenses involved, of course, would not be borne by the priest. For such reasons, temple finances were generally in good order.

K's household was well enough off. However, I don't know that they could have sent a second son to Tōkyō for schooling. I also don't know what role educational opportunities played in deciding K's adoption. At any rate, K was adopted into the physician's household. This was when we were still in middle school. I remember my surprise when the teacher called roll in class and K's family name had suddenly changed.

K's adoptive father was a wealthy man. K was provided with educational funding and came to Tōkyō. We didn't come to Tōkyō together, but after arriving we both took up lodgings in the same place. At that time, it was not uncommon to sleep and study two or three to a room. K and I took a room together. Like a pair of animals captured from the hillside and caged, we embraced each other within our confines and viewed the surroundings outside with suspicion. We were wary of Tōkyō and its people. Even so, from our six-mat room we dreamed about ruling the world.

We were quite serious. We had every intent of achieving greatness. K was especially driven. The word "devotion," harkening back to his temple upbringing, was constantly on his lips. And in all his deeds and actions, it seemed to me, devotion was duly embodied. Inwardly, I always held him in highest esteem.

From our middle school days, K would often stump me with difficult questions on religion or philosophy. It may be he was influenced by his father, or it may have been the rare air of the house into which he was born, a temple with its distinctive structures. At any rate, in comparison to your average priest, K came across as far more priest-like. K's adoptive family sent him to Tōkyō to learn medicine. K though, strong-willed in his thinking, came to Tōkyō resolved to not study medicine. Wasn't that the same thing, I asked him reprovingly, as defrauding his adoptive parents. He boldly affirmed that it was. It was a small price to pay, he said, for the sake of "the way." I don't think he really knew what he meant when he talked of "the way." I certainly can't say that I did. However, to us in our youth, these nebulous words rang sacred. Understanding aside, we proceeded forward in high-minded fervor, oblivious to any ignoble side to our actions. I thus came to support K in this views. I don't know how much difference my support made. Determined as he was, it's hard to imagine I could have dissuaded him through counterargument or objection. In encouraging him, though, I was fully aware, even in my youth, that I was taking a stake should things go awry. Even if I wasn't prepared for it at the time, it's always been clear to me in retrospect that my avid support implied a willingness to bear some share of the consequences.

Chapter 20

K and I enrolled in the same college. With his devil-may-care attitude, he proceeded to use the money from his foster family to pursue his own studies. I couldn't but conclude that there were two thoughts in his mind. The first was that they wouldn't find out, and the second was so-what-if-they-did. Between the two of us, K seemed the lesser concerned.

K didn't return home that first summer. He told me of his plans to rent a room at a temple in Komagome and study there. I returned in early September and, sure enough, found him holed up in a tumbledown temple near the Great Kannon. He had a small room off the main hall, where he seemed most content to study as he pleased. That was, I believe, when I first noticed how priest-like he'd become. He wore a ring of prayer beads on his wrist. I asked what they were for, and he showed me how he could count them off with his thumb. Each day, it seemed, he counted his way round and round the ring. I failed to see the significance of this. In counting beads round a ring, there was no end. At what point in his counting, or with what thought in his mind, did he bring his hand to a halt? This is a trifling point, but I often wondered nonetheless.

I saw that K had a Bible in his room. This surprised me. I'd known him to talk often of the sutras, but I'd never heard him express any interest in Christianity. I couldn't help but ask why he had it. He asked in return why he shouldn't. Any writing so cherished by so many was certainly worth a read. In addition, he wanted to read the Koran when he had a chance. He seemed fascinated by the concept of "Muhammad and the Sword."

In our second summer, K was called home. Even when home, he apparently made no mention of his field of study. His family, for their part, did not pick up on it. Having received a formal education yourself, you'll understand when I say that the larger world, when it comes to academic life, is woefully disinterested. What we take for common knowledge is fully opaque to others. We live in and breathe our own air, immersed in the ins and outs of academia, and we're prone to believe that the outside world takes notice. On this point, K was a more astute observer than myself, and thus ventured home without concern. We returned from the country together, and as soon as we boarded the train

I asked how things had gone. He replied that there was nothing worth reporting.

Our third summer was the one in which I turned my back on the land where my parents lay buried, resolved to never return. I had advised K that he should return home too, but he'd declined. He questioned the purpose of returning home each year. He found more value in staying put to study. Having no other recourse, I set off from Tōkyō alone. I've already written of how those months at home altered my destiny, so I won't revisit that story here. When I next saw K in September, my soul was brimming with discontent, melancholy, estrangement, and loneliness. K's destiny too, was in similar throes of its own. Unbeknownst to me, K had written to his adoptive family and confessed his deception. He told me he'd planned all along to do so. He may have figured that at this point, when it was too late to change course, they'd bless his choice and direct him to carry on. At any rate, he had no intention of deceiving his adoptive parents all the way into his graduate studies. Even had he wanted to, it was clear, no doubt, that deception had its limits.

Chapter 21

K's adoptive father was outraged at his letter. He fired back a severe reply. In light of such brazen parental deception, K was immediately disqualified from further financial support. K showed me this response. He also showed me a letter from his birth family that he'd received at about the same time. This one was no less scathing in its reproval. Perhaps in deference to his adoptive family, it stated clearly that he should expect no support from their side either. The question of whether K would be reinstated into his birth family or somehow negotiate to remain with his adoptive family was left for a future day. K's immediate problem now was how to get by from month to month.

I asked K for his thoughts on the matter. He said he would take a job, teaching night school or such. Things were simpler then than they are now, and finding a side job was not as hard as you might imagine. I didn't doubt that K could likely get by. However, I was also aware of my own obligation. When K had gone against his adoptive family and charted his own course, I'd come to support him in his decision. I couldn't just stand idly by. I immediately extended an offer of material assistance. K dismissed this offhand. In his mind, self-sufficiency was preferable by far to dependency on the patronage of a friend. Once in graduate school, he asserted, any man worth his salt should know how to fend for himself. I had no intention of wounding K's pride for the sake of my own satisfaction, so I withdrew and left him to his own means.

K soon found the kind of position he sought. However, to one who so cherished his time, it was clearly a burden. Despite the demands of his new job, he persevered and didn't let up on his studies. I worried about his health. Determined as he was, though, he laughed off my concerns and heeded me not in the least.

K's relationship with his adoptive family, all the while, grew more and more tumultuous. He no longer had the time to talk with me like before, so I didn't hear all the details, but I could see that any hope for resolution was slipping away. I knew that a certain someone had interceded with efforts toward conciliation. This someone wrote to K and urged him home. K, deciding the cause was already lost, did not comply. K's obstinacy—he explained that he could not return during the school year, but the other side still viewed it as obstinacy—seemed to just make bad things worse. His adoptive family was offended, and his birth family was angered as well. Out of concern, I wrote a letter in attempt to placate the parties, but to no avail. For my troubles they sent not a word in return. This bothered me greatly. Given the circumstances of the situation, I'd already been sympathetic to K. From that point on, objectivity be damned, I was fully in K's camp.

It was finally decided that K would be reinstated into his birth family. His birth family would reimburse his adoptive family for all monies applied toward his schooling. In exchange, his birth family was through with him. He was on his own from here on. To apply an archaic term, one could say that K had been disinherited. It may not have been quite that dire, but K himself saw it as such. K had grown up without his mother. Some facets of his character, it seemed, could be attributed to his upbringing under a stepmother. Had his real mother lived, I believe he might not have broken so severely from his birth family. His father, as I've already related, was a Buddhist priest. However, in his strict adherence to obligation, he came across as more warrior than priest.

Chapter 22

After K's situation had settled a bit, I received a long letter from the husband of his older sister. K's adoptive family were relatives of this man, and according to K his opinion had carried weight both in mediating the adoption and in later reversing it.

The letter asked for news on how K was faring. His sister was worried, it added, and could I please respond without delay. K was closer to this older sister, who had married into another family, than to his older brother who had succeeded his father at the temple. They were all three siblings of the same mother, but there was a significant gap in age between K and his sister. From his childhood, K's sister had been as a mother to him, more so than his stepmother.

I showed the letter to K. He seemed unsurprised and revealed to me that he'd received several such letters already from his sister. He said he'd written back that there was no need for concern. The family his sister had married into, unfortunately, was not well off. However sympathetic his sister might be, she was in no position to offer material assistance.

I wrote back to K's brother-in-law with a similar response as K's to his sister. I assured them, in no uncertain terms, that I would step in on K's behalf should the need arise. This was fully in fitting with my intent. In stating it so, I hoped to comfort K's sister who worried for his future. I also meant it as a rebuke against K's adoptive and birth families, whom I felt had disrespected me.

K was in the first year of his graduate studies when he was reinstated into his birth family. For the next year and a half, until around the middle of his second year, he supported himself through his own efforts. However, the toll this took on him was beginning to show, both physically and mentally. His troubles with his adoptive family, and the question of whether or not they would keep him, were also to blame. His sentiments were gradually getting the best of him. He sometimes talked as though all of humanity's sorrows were his to shoulder alone, and he would react most severely if challenged. He was irritated too by thoughts that his grand future, with so much potential, was slipping out of sight. When beginning academic endeavors, we all set out afresh with great ambitions. A year passes, then another, and graduation draws near. At this point, reality suddenly sets in, and most of us are disappointed in our own limitations. The same was true for K, but he took it so much harder than others. I finally decided I had to intervene.

I advised K to stop pushing himself so. I told him he'd find greater success in the long run by taking rest and engaging in leisure. Given K's obstinacy, I'd tempered my expectations from the start, but even at that I was unprepared for what I went through to finally persuade him. K asserted that his aim was more than just learning. He sought to fashion a mind of the strongest will. Austerity, he'd decided, was an essential means to this end. He was eccentric in this regard. His austere lifestyle, though, seemed not to be serving his will in the least. It was leading him, rather, toward a nervous breakdown. Finding no other recourse, I embraced his ideas with full-on empathy. I declared to him a like intention for my own life. (From my side, these were more than hollow words. K had a power of persuasion, and in expounding his views he'd begun to win me over.) I finally proposed that we room together to support each other in traversing the noble path.

To break his stubborn will, I threw myself at his feet. Only in so doing was I able to draw him in.

Chapter 23

Adjoining my room was a four-mat antechamber. Coming from the entry hall, one had to pass through this antechamber to reach my room, a situation that rendered it of little practical use. I put K in this room. My initial thought had been to place our desks together in my larger eight-mat room and reserve this smaller room for our shared use. K decided, though, that he preferred his own space, however cramped it might be, and chose to take the smaller room for his own.

As I've already noted, Okusan initially opposed these measures I sought to take. If she were running a boarding house, she said, then two would be better than one, and three would be better still. However, she was not in business, and she'd prefer that I drop the matter. I assured her she needn't worry, as K was not the burdensome type. Burdensome or not, she replied, he was fully unknown to her. When I countered reprovingly that I, her current lodger, had been no different, she did not back down but insisted she'd had a read on me from day one. I gave her an exasperated look. Then she changed her line of argument. For my own sake, I should not bring in K. I asked how this was for my own sake, and this time the look of exasperation was hers.

In all honesty, it was not essential that I room with K. However, had I doled out a monthly cash allowance before him, I firmly believed he would have refrained from accepting. He was too much the independent spirit. So I brought him into my home and discreetly paid Okusan the extra to cover his meals. At the same time, I made a point of not disclosing K's financial predicament to her.

I did make various mention of K's health and how, if left alone, he would only skew more eccentric. I also talked about K's failed relationship with his adoptive family and his estrangement from his birth family. In bringing in K, I informed her, I was prepared to embrace a drowning man and revive him with my own lifeblood. On that note, I implored both Okusan and her daughter to treat K with utmost kindness. At this point, Okusan was finally persuaded. K though, to whom I said nothing, was unaware of all this. I thought this for the best, and as he stolidly moved himself in, I welcomed him with a look of indifference.

Okusan and her daughter helped K settle in and attended kindly to his needs. Inwardly, I was well pleased, as I knew they were doing so in deference to me.—K, for his part, was his usual sullen self.

When I asked K how he liked his new surroundings, he replied simply that they weren't bad. As I saw things, this was quite the understatement. His previous place was a north-facing room. It was damp, musty, and filthy. And the board was no better than the room. For K, moving from there into my house was akin to coming out of a deep ravine to the top of a tall tree. His subdued response was in part due to his obstinacy and in part due to his tenets. Brought up as he was in Buddhist doctrine, he viewed anything beyond the essentials as extravagance and moral corruption. He was versed in the tales of virtuous priests and eminent saints of old, and he sought to separate the spirit from the flesh. He may have, at times, been wont to scourge his body for the betterment of his soul.

I took great care not to confront him. The best way to melt ice, I reasoned, was to set it out in the sun. In due time it would melt into warm water, and when it did it would react to its own transformation.

Chapter 24

In my own case, as a result of Okusan's care, the clouds hanging over my spirit had gradually cleared. I was aware of what had transpired, and now I sought the same effect for K. Having known K for many years, I knew that we were not of the same mettle. However, my own nerves had been soothed in this household, and I reasoned the place should work its same magic on K as well.

K was a man of greater resolve than myself. He studied twice as hard as I did, and he was blessed with a finer mind than my own. Our areas of study had diverged, but during our time together, in middle and high school, K was always the top student in the class. It was clear to me that I would never be his equal. However, in this time when I worked so to bring him into my home, I did believe myself the more sensible of us two. From my perspective, it seemed that K had lost sight of the difference between privation and perseverance. I write this especially for your sake, so please take note. Our faculties, whether those of the body or those of the mind, thrive or perish under external stimuli. In either case, it goes without saying that stimuli must increase over time. If one isn't careful, one can unwittingly, and unbeknownst even to those close by, steer oneself into great peril. Physicians will tell you there is nothing so indolent as the human stomach. Feed it only with gruel, they say, and it'll soon enough be incapable of anything solid. They advocate a diverse diet, but I think there's more to this than simply keeping in practice. It has to be the case, I also believe, that a gradual increase in stimuli be accompanied by a gradual increase in digestive resilience. Think of the consequences of the converse, if the stomach's faculty grew weaker with time, and I think you'll see my point. K was a greater man than myself, but he'd failed to grasp this truth. He seemed intent on living with hardship and making it his friend. He was convinced that through the virtues of repeated privation, he could one day embrace privation as his own.

I wished very much to enlighten K in such matters. It was a given, however, that he would only challenge my thoughts. No doubt, I reckoned, he would call up examples of great personages past. I on my part, then, would be compelled to point out that he and they were not the same. If he were amenable to such an idea, then that would be the end of it. Given his nature, though, having argued thus far he would not back down. He would push it further. He would shore up his words with actions. He would show himself a formidable man, not to be taken lightly. He would carry forward to his own detriment. In the end, he would only prevail in securing his own demise, but he would do so in grand fashion. Knowing his nature as I did, I had to hold my silence. Also, as I've noted before, from my perspective he seemed very close to a breakdown. If I did manage to argue him into submission, it would only serve to set him off. I wasn't one to shrink from a quarrel. However, when I thought back to my own situation, and the terrible isolation I'd felt, I was loathe to leave a close friend in such straits. I had no intention of pushing him further away. With this in mind, I refrained, even after he moved in with us, from doling out anything he might perceive as rebuke. I held my tongue and simply observed, waiting to see the effects of his new surroundings.

Chapter 25

Behind the scenes, I encouraged Okusan and her daughter to engage with K. His heretofore reticent lifestyle, I believed, was doing him great harm. I could only conclude that his heart, like steel left untouched, was showing signs of rust.

Okusan remarked with a laugh that she found him unapproachable. Her daughter offered up a specific example by way of illustration. When asked if he had coals in his hibachi, K had replied to her that he had none. When asked then if she should bring some, he'd declined, adding that there was no need. When asked if it wasn't cold, he'd acknowledged it was cold but stated again that he needed no coals. That had been the end of it. I couldn't just brush this off with a forced smile. I felt bad for her, and I did my best to try and smooth things over. It was springtime, and coals were by no means essential, but at the same time I could understand how the women were finding K difficult.

From then on, I did what I could to intervene in bringing K and the two women closer. If K and I were talking I would call one of them over. Or if I were with them in the same room I would pull in K. In either case, as the situation allowed, I worked to draw them closer. K, of course, did not appreciate my efforts. On one occasion, he abruptly rose and left the room. On another occasion, I called for him and he failed to appear. Where was the value, he asked, in idle chatter. I laughed this off, but I was all too aware of the contempt in his voice.

In some respects, K's contempt for me may have been justified. It could be argued that he'd set his sights much higher than mine. I wouldn't refute it. However, lofty goals, when coupled with day in and day out drudgery, make for the proverbial strange bedfellows. What he desperately needed, in my opinion, was a healthy dose of humanity. He could fill his head with images of great men, but to what purpose, I asked myself, if his own path to greatness were thwarted. His first lesson in humanity, I decided, should be exposure to the opposite sex. By exposing him to female company, I hoped to loose the rust from his lifeblood and see him renewed.

My efforts began to gradually bear fruit. What once seemed immiscible slowly started to mix. It seemed to dawn on K, bit by bit, that there existed a world outside of himself. He turned to me one day and conceded that women were not so contemptible after all. He had initially, it seemed, expected of women the same scholarship and learning he expected of me. Not finding it, he'd unleashed his contempt in response. He hadn't learned to adjust his approach based on gender. He'd observed every individual, man or woman, through the same lens. I pointed out to him that if the two of us, as men, exchanged ideas just among ourselves, we'd be fated forever to walking a single straight path. He readily acknowledged my point. At the time, smitten as I was with the daughter, it was natural for me to talk so. I did not, however, divulge these feelings to K.

I was elated to see K's heart, which he'd heretofore entombed in ramparts built from books, breaking out into the light. Such had been my aim from the start, and I couldn't help but feel the joy that comes with success. I didn't share these thoughts with K, but I did share them with Okusan and her daughter. Both seemed duly pleased.

Chapter 26

While K and I both studied in the same department, our areas of specialization were different, so it was only natural that our schedules should not coincide. When I came home early, I would simply pass through his empty room. When I came home late, I made it my habit to offer a simple greeting on the way to my room. K would always lift his eyes from his page and glance my way as I slid the partition aside. Then he would always ask if I'd just now returned. Sometimes I merely nodded in return, and at other times I voiced a simple affirmation as I passed on my way.

On one day, I had some business in Kanda and returned home much later than usual. I approached the gate at a quick pace and opened the latticework door with a clatter. At that same moment, I caught the sound of the daughter's voice. It seemed clearly to come from K's room. The hearth room and the daughter's room were straight back from the entry hall, in that order. To the left were K's room and my own. This was the lay of the house, and to one such as myself who'd been there a while, it was easy enough to know whose voice was coming from where. I closed the door behind me. As I did so, the daughter's voice immediately fell silent. As I removed my shoes—I wore stylish high-lace shoes at the time, which were quite a bother—as I was stooped over untying my laces, there was no sound at all from K's room. This struck me as odd. I wondered if I'd been imagining things. However, as I slid the partition aside for my usual passage through K's room, the two of them were, indeed, sitting there. K asked, as always, if I'd just now returned. The daughter welcomed me home from her spot on the floor. Maybe it was just in my mind, but her greeting somehow hit me as strained. I sensed something unnatural in her tone. I turned to her and asked after Okusan. I had no real reason for asking. I only did so because it seemed so still in the house.

Okusan, indeed, was away from the house. She had left with the maidservant. Consequently, K and the daughter were there on their own. This baffled me to no end. I'd been there a long time, and never once had Okusan gone out and left me alone with her daughter. I asked the daughter if something urgent had arisen. She merely laughed. I had a great dislike for women who laughed so in such situations. It may be a common fault among all young ladies, but this young lady seemed prone to find humor in every petty matter. One look at my face, however, was enough to bring her back to herself. It was nothing urgent, she told me sincerely, but a small errand had necessitated Okusan's absence. As a lodger, it was not my place to press any further. I held my silence.

I changed my clothes and had only just sat down when Okusan and the maidservant returned. After a bit, it was time to gather for dinner. When I'd first come in as a lodger, they'd treated me as a guest, with the maidservant bringing me my meals. After some time, they'd dispensed with formality and started calling me to join them. When K had moved in as a new lodger, I'd made a point of insisting that they treat him no differently. In exchange, I'd had a lightweight folding table made and presented it to Okusan. These are commonplace nowadays, but in those times it was unusual for family members to eat together around a table. I'd had to go all the way to a furniture maker in Ochanomizu, where I'd had it specially built to order.

At the table, Okusan explained that the fish vendor had not shown that day, and she'd had to go to town for our dinner. As I took this in and acknowledged it, the daughter looked at my face and again started laughing. Her laughter, however, was immediately shut down with a scolding from Okusan.

Chapter 27

A week later, I again found K and the daughter talking in his room. On this occasion, the daughter took one look at my face and burst out laughing. I perhaps should have asked her then and there what she found so amusing. Instead, I held my tongue and continued into my room. K had no chance to offer his usual greeting. The daughter, it seemed, soon thereafter opened the shōji and made her way back to the hearth room.

At dinner, the daughter remarked that I was eccentric. I refrained from asking what she meant. I simply watched as her mother threw her a reproving look.

After dinner, I invited K to join me for a stroll. We passed behind the Denzūin Temple, circled through the botanical garden lanes, and emerged at the bottom of Tomizaka. It was by no means a short stroll, but we talked very little. K, by nature, was even more reserved than I was. I'm hardly the talkative type, but I did my best to engage him as we walked. Foremost on my mind was the family with whom we lodged. I wanted to know K's thoughts on Okusan and her daughter. All of his answers, however, were evasive and noncommittal. He spoke in simple terms yet still remained elusive. His mind seemed much more focused on his studies than on the two women. Our second year exams, of course, were just around the corner, and between the two of us, as any objective observer could readily have concluded, K was the serious student. He duly impressed me with references to Emanuel Swedberg and such, of whom I knew very little.

When our exams were successfully behind us, Okusan congratulated us and noted that we both had just one more year to go. For Okusan's part, the graduation of her daughter, in whom she placed great pride, was just around the corner. K remarked to me how women finish their schooling yet still don't know anything. The daughter's extracurricular activities, her lessons in needlework, koto, flower arrangement and such, were entirely lost on K. I chided him for his oversight. I repeated to him my prior argument that he was looking in the wrong place and his critique of women was misguided. He didn't refute my words, but he didn't embrace them either. I was happy to see this. Judging from his manner, he still viewed women with contempt. And he seemed to take little interest in the daughter of the house, who to me exemplified the female gender. I can say looking back now that, at that time, I was already jealous of K.

I suggested to K that we travel together over the summer. His response was unenthusiastic. He was, of course, in no position to travel of his own accord. On the other hand, there was nothing to prevent him from accompanying me at my request. I asked him why he was reluctant to go. He replied that there was no deep reason. He just preferred to stay home and read. When I contended that it was better to escape the heat and study somewhere cool, he replied that I was welcome to do so alone. I had no intention of leaving that house without K. I was uneasy with how close he had grown to the family. You may object that I was uncomfortable now with the very outcome I'd desired from the start. I'll concede I was acting the fool. Okusan, seeing our discussion go nowhere, felt compelled to intervene. It was finally settled that the two of us would travel to Bōshū.

Chapter 28

K was not the traveling type. It was the first time for me, too, in Bōshū. Not knowing the territory, we climbed ashore where the boat made first land. I believe that was Hota. I don't know how it might have changed since, but in those days it was an utterly wretched fishing village. The whole place reeked of fish. Each time in the sea, we were beaten down by the waves, emerging with scrapes on our hands and feet. Fist-sized stones were tossed about by the breakers there in a never-ending churn.

I'd soon had enough. K said nothing, however, either for or against the place. His face, too, was pure indifference. At the same time, he seldom came back unscathed from the sea. Finally, at my urging, we moved on to Tomiura. From Tomiura, we went to Nako. The entire coast was a gathering place for students back then, so wherever we went a suitable bathing beach awaited. K and I would perch ourselves on the rocks above the shore and gaze at the color of the distant sea or survey the shallows. From our vantage on the rocks, the views of the water were splendid. Small fish of crimson or indigo, colors not seen in the marketplace, were on brilliant display as they darted about in the clear waves.

I often had a book open before me. K was wont to just sit there in silence. For all I knew, he may have been deeply pensive, may have been drinking in the sights, or may have been daydreaming fancifully. I sometimes lifted my gaze to ask what he was doing. He simply replied that he was doing nothing. I often thought how nice it would be if the young lady of our house, rather than K, were the one seated quietly beside me. That in itself was fine, but I also suspected on occasion that K, as he sat there on those rocks, might perhaps be harboring exactly the same wish.

In those moments, my appetite for quiet reading would suddenly disappear. I'd abruptly jump to my feet and yell with abandon at the top of my lungs. I lacked the composure to bring forth any studied verse or intelligible tune. All I could do was scream like a savage. On one occasion I seized K's neck from behind. What would he do, I asked, if I pushed him off and into the sea. He didn't stir. His back still to me, he replied that it would suit him fine, that I should go ahead and do it. I immediately withdrew my hands from his neck.

K's frayed nerves, by that time, seemed to be greatly improved. My own, in contrast, were more and more on edge. Seeing K so self-assured, I couldn't help but envy him. I loathed him too. Maybe it was his evident disinterest in my affairs. I saw this disinterest as a sign of his newfound confidence. This confidence he showed by no means warmed my heart. My doubts had the best of me, and I needed to know what lay behind it. Had he recovered his old optimism, his sense of a bright future to be gained through study and exertion? If it were just that, then his and my interests were in no way at odds. In fact, I should feel pleased for having helped him so. However, if his peace of mind involved the young lady of our house, then I would never forgive him. Oddly enough, he seemed fully unaware of my affection toward her. Of course, I was not one to parade my passions. And K, by his nature, was obtuse in such regards. It was partly for this reason that I had brought him into the house without concern.

Chapter 29

I thought to open up and tell K everything. This wasn't the first time, of course, that I'd had this thought. I'd harbored such intent in advance of our travel but had been unable to find or create the right opportunity. Looking back now, my acquaintances of those days were a curious lot. In conversation, the topic of women was never broached. There were many, no doubt, who had no experience to draw on, but even those who did, it seemed, routinely held their tongues. To your generation, who breathe a freer air, this must certainly seem odd. Perhaps we were slaves to the ethics of times past, or perhaps we were fettered by inhibition. I leave it to you to judge.

K and I could discuss anything. Love and romance were no exception. They didn't fail to come up on occasion, but they came up as abstractions, and we always fell to theorizing. And even this was only seldom. Our discourse, for the most part, was occupied by talk of books, or studies, or our future livelihoods, or our aspirations, or of ways to cultivate one's mind. However close we might have been, there was no breaking through the dispassionate tone of those days. The bond between us was premised on dispassion. Since resolving that I should disclose to K my feelings for the young lady, I'd been tormented time and again by awkward indecision. I wished that just once I could pry open his head and pass a tender breath into his mind.

Things that to you may seem fully absurd, were to me, at that time, a source of genuine consternation. During our travels, just as at home, I was overly timid. My eyes were always on K, watching for a chance, but I was helpless against his highbrow demeanor. It was as if, to my mind, his heart were hard-coated with a heavy coat of black lacquer. The passion I sought to pour out would only be repelled. His heart would accept not a drop.

There were times when K's rugged and distant demeanor reassured me. At those times, I would scold myself for harboring suspicions and apologize to K in my mind. While growing apologetic toward K, I regarded myself as a lowlife, and I was hit with a sudden sense of shame. Before long, though, my prior suspicions would return with a vengeance, commanding my thoughts and skewing everything to my own disadvantage. K's looks, it seemed, were the kind that women favored. Unlike my own fidgety disposition, his demeanor was appealing to the opposite sex. What faults he had, he compensated for with rugged masculinity, appearing superior, on the whole, to myself. Our areas of study were different, but I knew, of course, that I could never match him in scholarship.—All his merits assaulted my thoughts at once, and my brief assurance soon gave way to anxiety.

Seeing me so unsettled, K suggested we should return to Tōkyō if I wasn't enjoying myself. This steeled my resolve to stay. The truth, perhaps, was that I didn't want K back in Tōkyō. We circled the Bōshū headland and emerged on the opposite side. Under a blistering sun, we forced ourselves on through Kazusa, whose modest distances proved deceptively arduous. I saw no purpose anymore in trudging so. I voiced this half-jokingly to K. He stated in response that we were born with feet, and thus we walk. He added that we should cool ourselves in the sea, and he didn't hesitate to do so, regardless of place or time. Afterward, though, the merciless sun would beat us back down, leaving us languid and worn.

Chapter 30

Walking on thus, worn down in the heat, one begins in time to feel out of sorts. It's not as though one is ill. It's as though one's soul were suddenly cast into an unfamiliar body. I conversed with K as always, but it seemed somehow different. The intimacy and enmity I felt toward him took on a special constitution, a flavor of the road as it were. In short, the heat, the salt, the waves, and the walking established a connection between us heretofore unknown. We were like a pair of traveling merchants fallen together on the road. We talked at length, but touched not once on our usual weighty topics.

We continued on in this manner to Chōshi, with just one exception that left on me a lasting impression. Before leaving Bōshū, we stopped at a place called Kominato and toured Tai no Ura. It's been many years now, and I didn't take much interest in it at the time, but they say that Nichiren was born there. Legend has it that on the day of his birth, two tai were tossed up onto the shore. Since that day, the local fishermen have refrained from taking tai, and they've thrived in the bay there. We hired a small boat and set out to view them.

I was intent the whole while on watching the waves. My eyes were transfixed by the site of the tai, tinged in purple, darting through the surf. K, however, failed to share my interest. His mind, it seemed, was less on the tai and more on Nichiren. There was a temple nearby called Tanjōji. It was no doubt named so in honor of Nichiren's birth, and its buildings were grand. K proposed that we stop there and call on the priest.

To tell the truth, we were a strange-looking pair. This was especially true of K, who had lost his hat to the sea in a strung gust and was wearing a bamboo replacement he'd purchased along the way. Our clothes, of course, were filthy, and on top of that we both reeked of sweat. I suggested we shouldn't go meet with the priest. K was obstinate and wouldn't hear it. If I didn't want to go with, he said, then I could wait for him outside. Seeing no better alternative, I accompanied him through the entryway, thinking to myself we'd likely be turned away. Priests, however, are surprisingly civil. We were shown to a grand parlor and promptly joined there. K and I had dissimilar interests at the time, and I only half listened to his conversation with the priest. K wanted to know all about Nichiren. The priest explained how Nichiren was so skilled in the grass script that he was known as "grass Nichiren." I still remember K, who's own brushwork was sub-par, returning a dismissive look. He wanted something more, something of deeper significance. I don't know that the priest managed to satisfy him, but once outside the grounds he turned to me and began to expound on Nichiren. I was too worn down by the heat to care much. I simply humored him with mechanical replies. When these became burdensome, I stopped responding altogether.

It was on the following evening, if I remember right, after we'd reached our inn, dined, and were preparing for bed, when our conversation suddenly took a sour turn. K was still fuming from the prior day, when he'd tried to engage me on Nichiren and I'd responded with disinterest. Those who don't seek to better the spirit, he remarked, are mere simpletons. He was clearly rebuking me, implying that I was fickle. My spirit at the time, however, was occupied with thoughts of the daughter of our house, and I wasn't about to let his disrespect go unchallenged. I took up my own defense.

Chapter 31

I used the word "humanity" extensively. K contended that I was using this word as cover for my own shortcomings. Looking back later, I could see that he'd been right. My purpose in using it, however, had been to force K to confront his own deficiency. Having once charted this argumentative course, I could not readily retreat. I asserted my opinion all the more forcefully. K asked in return where it was that I found him lacking in humanity. I told him—"You're human enough. Maybe too human. But your words, and your actions too, are void of humanity."

When I told him this, he didn't refute it. He simply replied that if he did come across so, it was only because he had not yet mastered his own soul. I began to feel bad for him, and this served to disarm me. I pressed the matter no further. K grew more and more somber. He remarked, with a tinge of sadness, that if I knew those men of old, like he did, I would not censure him so. The men of old he referred to were neither heroes nor great achievers. They were sufferers, men who tormented their flesh and scourged their bodies for the sake of their souls. K added with disappointment that I didn't understand how he himself had suffered so in order to walk in their shoes.

K and I left it at that and slept. From the following morning, we were once again like traveling merchants, sweating as we trudged on our way. However, I often thought back on that evening as we journeyed along. I'd been presented the ultimate opportunity, and I regretted greatly that I hadn't seized it. It occurred to me that instead of abstract talk on humanity, I should have divulged to K in simple terms the things I was feeling.

In fact, my fixation on "humanity" was indeed grounded in my feelings for the daughter of our house. Instead of assaulting K's ears with theories distilled from that truth, I'd have been better served in revealing it to him directly. The bond between us, however, was built on erudition, and it had come to possess its own form of inertia. I'll confess here that I lacked the courage to upset that inertia. I didn't dare to perturb it with sentiment. I could say that pretentiousness got the better of me, or I could say that vanity worked its mischief. Please note that I use the terms "pretentiousness" and "vanity" here in not quite their usual sense. As long as you understand my meaning, then with that I'm content.

We returned to Tōkyō burnt black by the sun. By that time my demeanor had changed. I had lost all interest in splitting hairs over what was or wasn't humanity. K too had shed his sage-like aura. By that time, I expect, his thoughts were free from problems of the spirit and problems of the flesh. Like aliens with darkened faces, we watched as Tōkyō teemed with motion around us. At Ryōgoku, despite the heat, we dined on game fowl. Newly energized, K suggested we walk home to Koishikawa. I could generally better him in matters of physical endurance, so I readily agreed.

Okusan was shocked at the sight of us when we arrived home. In addition to our dark complexions, we were both gaunt from our endless trekking. All the same, Okusan complimented us on how fit we both looked. The daughter couldn't help but laugh at her mother's glaring inconsistency. Her laughter, though, which had annoyed me on occasion prior to our journey, this time brightened my mood. Perhaps because of the circumstance, or perhaps due to our long absence.

Chapter 32

On another front, I perceived a subtle shift in the young lady's manner. In returning home from a long journey and resuming normal routine, there were many things that required a woman's care. Okusan and her daughter both helped us out, but the young lady seemed to be treating me with preference over K. Had she done this overtly, I might have been uncomfortable. I think it likely, in that case, I'd have found occasion to object. In this regard, though, I was happy to note how she carried it off with perfection. That is to say, she apportioned her grace in my favor, but in subtle ways that only I would notice. As a result, K was none the wiser, and he showed no signs of resentment. I'd gained the upper hand, and a song of triumph rang through my mind.

Summer finally passed, and in mid-September we resumed our studies. K and I once again came and went according to our respective schedules. Three days a week, I returned home later than he did, but not once did I see any further instance of the young lady visiting his room. He would glance my direction as always, and ask if I'd just now come home. I would give in return a simple, mechanical nod, fully devoid of meaning.

One morning, I think around mid-October, I overslept and rushed off to school in Japanese dress. I didn't have time for my high-lace shoes, so I jumped into my straw sandals and darted out. According to our schedules, my return home should have preceded K's. That being the case, I pushed opened the latticework entry door with a clatter. As I did so, I was surprised by the sound of K's voice. At the same time, the young lady's laughter reached my ears. I didn't have to deal with my usual shoes, so I immediately entered the house and slid aside the partition. The young lady, however, was already gone.

I caught just a flash of her back side, a retreating figure that seemed to take flight from K's room. I asked K why he was back so soon. He told me hadn't been feeling well and had stayed home. I went to my own room and sat down, and before long the young lady appeared with tea. It was then that she finally welcomed me home. A world-wise man would have smiled and asked why she'd run away. I didn't do this. Inside, though, the matter weighed on me heavily. After a moment, she rose and returned via the veranda. However, she paused in front of K's room and exchanged a few words with him through the partition. This was some continuation of their previous conversation. Not having been privy to what preceded, I couldn't follow what they were talking of now.

Over time, the young lady grew more and more nonchalant. Even when K and I were both in the house, she would approach his room from the veranda and call his name. Then she would visit with him at leisure. At times, of course, she was giving him his mail or returning his laundered clothes. Such interaction between two people in the same house was by no means unreasonable. To one such as myself though, who so strongly desired to possess this young lady exclusively, the extent of their interaction was excessive. It even seemed to me, at times, that she was avoiding me to frequent K's room. You may wonder why I didn't just turn K out. I'd invested great effort to bring him in, and were I to turn him out, my efforts would all come to naught. I couldn't let this happen.

Chapter 33

It was a day in November, when a cold rain was falling. I returned home by my usual route, cutting through the Konnyaku Enma temple and ascending the narrow lane. My overcoat was dripping with rain. K's room was empty, but his brazier glowed warmly with a newly kindled flame. Eager to warm my cold hands over coals, I quickly slid aside the partition to my own room. I found a cold brazier with nothing but pale ash. No fire remained. Discontent washed over me.

It was Okusan who heard me come in and came to greet me. She saw me standing in silence in the middle of the room, and she was kind enough to help me out of my coat and into Japanese attire. When I told her I was cold, she went into the next room and returned with K's brazier. I asked if K was already home, and she told me he'd come back and then departed again. This was a day when K's schedule had him coming home later than me, and I gave her a puzzled look. She supposed he must have had some business to attend to.

I sat for a while and read. The house was silent, with no voice to be heard. Early winter's cold and dreary sting was palpable. I immediately put aside my book and rose to my feet. I needed to get to livelier quarters. The rain had finally lifted, but the sky still weighed heavy, like cold lead. I shouldered my umbrella as a precaution and headed out. I moved east along the earthen wall in back of the armory, descending the hill. This was in the days before the roads were improved, and their pitch was much steeper than now. The road was narrow, and by no means straight. At the bottom, tall buildings flanked the south side, hindering the drainage of water, and the road was awash in mud. The narrow span between the stone bridge and the Yanagi-chō thoroughfare was worst of all.

Even those in stilted sandals or high boots were forced to tread carefully. All were intent on adhering tightly to a narrow path down the middle of the lane, a place from which the mud had been pushed away to either side by the foot traffic. The width of this narrow path was no more than half a meter, so it was almost like walking on a ribbon that had been unfurled down the lane. All moved slowly, and in single file. Walking this ribbon, I suddenly encountered K. I'd been preoccupied with my feet, and I didn't notice his presence until we were face to face. Only in the moment when I found my way blocked and happened to lift my gaze did I first recognize him standing there. I asked him where he'd been, and he replied simply that he'd just been out for a bit. The manner of his reply was terse as always. K and I maneuvered around each other on the narrow ribbon. As we did so, I saw there was a young lady behind him. I'm nearsighted, so it wasn't apparent to me at first, but after moving past K and seeing her face, I was quite surprised to recognized her as the young lady of our house. She greeted me with a slight blush on her cheeks. Hairstyles then were different than today, with no extending brim. Instead, her hair was coiled like a serpent over the center of her head. I gazed vacantly at her hair for a moment, before realizing that one of us would have to yield the way to the other. Resolutely, I stuck one foot in the muck, making way for her to pass with relative ease.

    I continued on to the Yanagi-chō thoroughfare, but from there had no idea where to go next. Nothing was of any interest. I tramped through the mud with abandon, paying no heed where it splashed. Then I turned and headed home.

Chapter 34

I asked K if he and the young lady had gone out together. He told me that wasn't the case. He'd met her by chance in Masago-chō, he explained, and accompanied her back home. I could find no opening for querying further. However, I couldn't resist asking the same question of the young lady at dinner. She responded with that laugh of hers that I so disliked. Then she asked me to guess where she'd been. My temper was short in those days, and I didn't take kindly to her trifling with me. Of those at the table, though, only Okusan seemed to notice this. K was fully indifferent. As for the young lady's attitude, I couldn't decide whether she was provoking me intentionally or merely knew no better. She was more discrete than most of her peers, but she was not immune to the common flaws or her cohort. Moreover, these flaws seemed more apparent since K had entered the house. I wasn't sure whether to attribute this to my jealousy of K or to her toying with my emotions. I have no intention, even now, of denying the jealousy I harbored at the time. As I've noted many times, I was keenly aware of these other emotions that lurk alongside affection. Furthermore, these other emotions were easily triggered by occasions that, to an impartial observer, were nothing at all. If I may digress a bit, it seems to me that jealousy may well be the reverse side of affection. Since marrying, I've felt this feeling slowly lose its grasp. At the same time, my affection too is no longer as intense as it once was.

I thought I might thrust my heart, till now so indecisive, with full abandon into the other party's bosom. By other party, I refer here not to the young lady in question, but Okusan. I thought to ask Okusan outright for her daughter's hand. Having resolved to do so, however, I failed, day after day, to act. In hearing this, you may well view me as spineless. That's fine if you do, but you should understand that my failure in action did not arise from weakness of intention. Before K's arrival, dread of deception had held me in check, precluding any initiative. After K moved in, I was shackled by misgivings, wondering if the young lady didn't perhaps prefer him over me. If she did prefer him then there would be no point, I concluded, in professing my affection. It wasn't so much fear of losing face. However I might yearn for her, if she deep down cherished another, then I was loathe to have her. There are men in this world who will happily wed the woman they fancy by hook or by crook. Such men, I believed at that time, were nothing other than ruffians tainted by worldly wear. Either that or they were dullards to whom the finer points of love were beyond reach. In my passion, I rejected the line of reasoning that a bride once taken would warm to one over time. In short, I subscribed to the theory of noble love. At the same time, I was hopelessly circumspect in pursuing of such love.

Over the course of our time together, I had ample opportunity to bare my soul directly to the young lady in question, but I took care not to. That this ran counter to the conventions of Japanese society was firmly ingrained in my mind. This wasn't, however, the only thing that restrained me. I was convinced that no Japanese woman, much less a young lady, would dare to speak candidly under such circumstances. Her feelings, no doubt, would be veiled by words of deference.

Chapter 35

Thus I stood, frozen in place, incapable of movement in any direction. There are times when one is unwell and requires rest. The eyes alone are alert, and all around is plain to see, but the hands and feet are utterly void of volition. Unbeknownst to others, I often felt a similar form of distress.

The old year drew to a close, and New Year's was upon us. One day, Okusan asked K to bring a friend over for karuta. She was taken aback when K promptly replied that he had no friends. In fact, there really was no one whom he could truly call a friend. There were those whom he greeted in passing on the street, but that by no means implied that he was close enough to invite them over for games. Okusan tried again with me, asking if I could invite someone I knew. Regrettably, I was in no mood for merrymaking. I sidestepped her request, giving a noncommittal and lukewarm response. However, when evening came both K and I were coerced out by the young lady of the house. Playing karuta with just us members of the household, and no guests, the scene was quite subdued. Furthermore, K was unaccustomed to games and could do no better than observe idly. I asked him if he even knew the hundred karuta verses. He replied that he really didn't. The young lady, apparently, decided I was deriding him. Thereafter, she made a point of coming to his assistance. In the end, the two were like a team, with me as their chosen adversary. One false move from K, and I would have confronted them both with harsh words. Fortunately though, his manner was unaffected. There was no show of triumph in his demeanor, and the situation passed without incident.

A few days later, Okusan and her daughter left home in the morning, telling us they were off to visit a relative in Ichigaya. Classes hadn't resumed yet, so K and I remained behind as house sitters. I didn't feel like reading, nor like taking a stroll, so I simply rested my elbows on the edge of the brazier, propped my chin in my palms, and allowed my mind to wander. There was no sound from K, who was in the adjoining room. It was so quiet that neither registered the other's presence. This was nothing out of the ordinary for us, and I didn't give it a second thought.

Around ten, K suddenly opened the fusuma and appeared before me. Standing on the threshold, he asked what I was thinking about.

I hadn't really been thinking about anything. Or if I had been, then I suppose the young lady of the house, as usual, was the object of my musings. If I were dwelling on her, then I was also dwelling on Okusan, and my thoughts of the ladies, of late, were no longer separable from K himself, whom I couldn't push out of the picture. I'd come to regard K, in some sense, as a nuisance, but I couldn't very well report this to his face. Rather, I continued to look back at him in silence. As I did so, he determinedly entered my room and seated himself before the brazier. I immediately removed my elbows from the edge and nudged it a bit in his direction.

Uncharacteristically, K initiated conversation. Where in Ichigaya, he wondered, had Okusan and her daughter gone. I told him I thought they were visiting an aunt. K asked in turn who this aunt was. I informed him that this aunt, too, was married to a military man. Then he asked why they'd gone so soon, as women customarily waited until the fifteenth before making New Year's rounds. All I could say to this was that I didn't know.

Chapter 36

K kept on with questions about Okusan and her daughter. In the end, he probed beyond my capacity to answer. Rather than bother me, his probing struck me as curious. Thinking back on the times I'd tried to engage him on the topic of the ladies, I couldn't help but notice the shift in his manner. I finally asked him why suddenly, on this day, he was so interested. He immediately fell silent. However, I could see the flesh around his closed lips quivering. He was reticent by nature. When he was thinking to say something, he would always chew his words over first. When his lips defied his will and refused to open, it meant he was pondering weighty words. Then, when his voice finally broke free, it would roar forth with twofold force.

As I watched his mouth, I could tell that something was coming, but I had no idea what. Hence I was blindsided. Imagine my surprise when he opened his mouth and solemnly professed a heartrending love for the young lady of the house. I instantly froze, as though he'd cast a spell and turned me to stone. I emitted not a murmur. My mouth lost all faculty for speech.

You could say that my being was reduced to pure dread, or perhaps it was pure anguish. At any rate, I was reduced to a single emotion. Like stone or like steel, I went rigid from head to toe. I was too rigid to even draw a breath. Fortunately, I wasn't long in this state. A moment later, I'd regained my sensibilities. The first thing I did was kick myself. I realized I'd been beaten.

At the time, an appropriate response eluded me entirely. I expect I lacked the capacity to even consider one. Even as a clammy sweat seeped from my armpits and into my shirt, I sat there stoically, without stirring. K continued on in his signature solemn voice, pouring his heart out a bit at a time. My anguish was unbearable. I imagine this anguish must have been written across my face, like the bold clear print on a large handbill, for all to see. Even K should have seen it clearly, but he was too absorbed in his own affair to lend me any regard. His confession continued on, from beginning to end, in the same vein. It was slow and heavy, and it impressed me thus as firmly rooted, not something easily dismissed. My thoughts were in a frenzy, wondering what I should do, and I only half listened to his words. The details of what he said might just as well have fallen on deaf ears, but the tone with which he spoke reverberated forcefully through my being. In addition to the anguish I've described, I began to also sense a certain kind of fear. In short, the fear of facing a stronger rival was starting to grip my mind.

When K finished speaking, I had nothing to say in response. My silence wasn't one of calculation. I wasn't weighing whether I should best counter with a similar confession or keep my feelings hidden. I simply had nothing to say. Nor did I feel any desire to speak.

When it was time for lunch, K and I sat face to face at the table. The maidservant waited on us. Never had I experienced a less appetizing meal. The two of us exchanged hardly a word. We didn't know when Okusan and her daughter would return.

Chapter 37

We withdrew to our respective rooms and saw each other no more. K was as quiet as he'd been all morning.

I was lost in thought.

It did occur to me, of course, that I should open myself to K. At the same time, though, I felt that I'd missed my chance. It seemed to me now that I'd failed grandly. Why had I not been able to stop him, to cut him off and counter him? I should at least have followed his example and related, without hesitation, my own feelings. Now that the moment had passed, to broach the subject anew seemed awkward. I could think of no way forward. My head was swimming in regret.

I hoped that K might open the partition and engage me again. As I saw it, he'd blindsided me earlier. I'd been caught unprepared. My heart now schemed how to recoup the morning's loss. From time to time I lifted my gaze to the fusuma. I looked in vain, however, as it never moved. K held his silence.

After a time, the silence began working mischief in my mind. I wondered, in desperation, what K was thinking on his side of the partition. Ordinarily, we lived in our own silent worlds, with only this thin partition between us. Under usual circumstances, the quieter he kept the less I sensed his presence. It's fair to say, though, that at this time I was far from my usual self. Even so, I couldn't bring myself to open the fusuma from my side. Having once missed my chance, there was nothing to do but wait to be re-engaged.

I finally found myself unable to stay still. The longer I held my ground, the greater my urge to burst in on K. I had to get up, and after doing so I made my way onto the veranda. From there I went to the hearth room and, having nothing better to do, poured out a cup of hot water from the iron kettle and sipped it. Then I went to the entry hall. Having gone to great lengths to avoid K's room, I now found myself out on the street. There was nowhere, of course, that I needed to go. I was there because I couldn't stay still. I wandered aimlessly through the town, regarding its New Year's adornments. However much I wandered, my thoughts remained on K. Shaking him off was not the intent of my stroll. On the contrary, I was set, as I wandered, on coming to grips with who he was.

First of all, he struck me as enigmatic. Why had he hit me out of the blue with such a revelation? And how could it be he'd fallen so hard as to have no choice but to confess? Had his former self been thoroughly swept away? The answers to all of these questions eluded me. I knew him as iron-willed. I knew him as earnest. There was much more about him, though, that I felt I needed to learn. Only then could I determine how to approach him. At the same time, I was strangely unsettled by the thought that we should be rivals. As I wandered the town in a daze, I pictured him in my mind's eye, sitting there quietly in his room. A voice in my head told me I walked in vain, that I had no power to affect K. Perhaps in my mind he was larger than life, monstrous. I had a sense, even, that he would torment me all my days.

I returned home exhausted. K was quiet as ever. There was no sound at all from his room.

Chapter 38

Shortly after my return, I caught the sound of a rickshaw. Wheels back then weren't rubberized like they are now. They made a terrible racket, and it carried for quite some distance. Finally, the cart came to a halt before our gate.

I was called to dinner some thirty minutes later. The adjacent room was colored by bright clothing that Okusan and her daughter had hastily thrown off on their return. They had hurried home, they said, to prepare us a timely dinner. Their effort, however, was largely in vain. I sat at the table like a man guarding his words, offering only curt responses. K was even more reticent still. Our moods were in sharp contrast to those of the two ladies who, having made a rare outing together, had returned in the best of spirits. Okusan asked me if something was wrong. I told her I was feeling a bit out of sorts. I was, in fact, feeling out of sorts. The daughter, in turn, asked the same thing of K. K didn't follow suit and say he was out of sorts. He simply said that he didn't feel like talking. She asked him why he didn't feel like talking. In that moment, I perked up my heavy eyelids and looked his way. I wanted to know how he would respond. His lips, as they were wont to do, trembled a bit. To the unknowing eye, it could only seem that he was stuck for an answer. The daughter smiled and remarked that he must be lost again in his thoughts. K's face reddened a shade.

That evening I went to bed early. I'd said at dinner that I wasn't feeling well, and Okusan, concerned, came to my room around ten with soba broth. My room, however, was fully in darkness. She remarked her surprise as she cracked the fusuma a bit. Light from K's desk lamp pierced the darkness at an angle. Apparently he was still up. Okusan seated herself at my bedside. She thought I must have caught cold and, saying that I should warm myself, she pushed a cupful of broth my way. I had no choice but to down the thick broth in her presence.

I ruminated in the darkness until it grew late. Of course I was chasing the same problem in circles, getting nowhere. Suddenly, I felt the need to know what K was doing in the adjacent room. Half unconsciously, I called out to him. From the other room, he called back. He was still awake. Through the partition, I asked if he hadn't gone to bed yet. He answered simply that he was about to. I asked next what he was doing. There was no answer. Instead, I clearly discerned, five or six minutes later, the sound of his closet opening and the sound of him laying out his bedding. I called out again to ask what the time was. He replied that it was twenty past one. After that, I heard him blow out his lamp, and all in the house was dark and still.

There in the darkness, though, my eyes were open wide. Still only half consciously, I called out to K again. He called back in the same manner as before. Finally broaching the subject, I asked if we could further our conversation of that morning. I had no intention, of course, of talking through the partition, but I expected at least his agreement. His response this time, however, was not so forthcoming. He murmured back quietly, his voice steeped in reluctance. I was seized with a sense of dread.

Chapter 39

K's tepid response was reflected in his behavior the next day and the day after. He showed no interest in touching on the subject at hand. Then again, the chance didn't present itself. Unless Okusan and her daughter left the house for the day, the two of us couldn't talk heart to heart or at length. I was keenly aware of this.

I was aware of this, but agitated nonetheless. As a result, I changed my tact. I'd been scheming in the shadows, waiting for K to approach me, but I decided now to broach the subject myself at first chance.

At the same time, I carefully observed the members of the household. I saw nothing out of the ordinary, however, in either Okusan's manner or in her daughter's bearing. If there was no notable change in their behavior following K's confession, then I had to conclude that he'd only confessed to me. It seemed certain that the crucial person in question and Okusan, who was effectively her caretaker, were still unaware. This thought helped calm my mind. If that were the case, then I didn't need to rush things. Rather than force the conversation, I decided to bide my time and seize the opportunity when it arose. I let the matter lie for a while.

As I've described this, it may sound simple, but my heart heaved through myriad highs and lows in the process, akin to the ebb and flow of the tides. I kept my eye on K, and I assigned various significance to his lack of initiative. I observed the words and actions of Okusan and her daughter, and in the end I couldn't help but question their authenticity. I wondered if the complex mechanisms at work in the human heart were capable, like the hands of a clock on a numbered face, of faithful outward expression. In short, you should understand that I satisfied myself only after multiple fits and starts. In all honesty, "satisfied" is hardly the right word to apply here.

Before long, classes resumed. On days when our schedules coincided, K and I left the house together. Whenever possible, we walked home together too. To an outside observer, we would seem close as ever. Deep down, however, we were no doubt each scheming in our own separate worlds. One day, as we walked on the street, I suddenly confronted K. My first question was whether his confession of the other day was to me alone, or whether he had also conveyed his feelings to Okusan and her daughter. My approach henceforth, I'd decided, hinged on his answer to this question. He assured me that he'd confided in on one else. The situation was as I'd surmised, and in my heart I was duly elated. I knew that between the two of us, K was the more brazen. I could never match him in audacity. Strangely, though, at the same time I trusted him. He'd let his adoptive family fund his education for three years under false pretenses, but this, in my eyes, in no way diminished his credibility. On the contrary, I admired him all the more. Despite my distrust of humanity, I readily took him at his word.

I turned to him again and asked where he intended to go with his feelings. What I wanted to know was whether his confession was the end of the matter or, having confessed, did he hope to take things further to fruition. On this point, though, he provided no answer. With downcast eyes, he resumed walking. I beseeched him to keep no secrets, to tell me everything. He answered simply that he had nothing to keep from me. The information I sought, however, did not cross his lips. We were standing in the road, and I couldn't hold my ground indefinitely. For the time being, I let it go.

Chapter 40

One day I found myself, for the first time in a long while, in the school library. I sat at the corner of a large table, sunlight from the window warming half of my body, flipping through a newly-arrived foreign periodical. My instructor had assigned me a research topic in my area of study that was due the next week.

Not finding the information I needed, I'd been back and forth with several different periodicals. In the end, I'd finally found a relevant article and begun reading intently. At that moment, from across the large table, I was quietly called by name. I lifted my eyes, and there was K. He leaned over the table and brought his face close to mine. As you well know, a loud voice that disrupts others is not allowed in the library, so there was nothing unusual in K's behavior. Nevertheless, on this occasion it somehow struck me as odd.

K asked in a quiet voice if I was studying. I told him I had a small research assignment. Continuing in the same quiet tone, he asked if I'd join him for a walk. I answered that I could walk with him if he waited a bit. He said he would wait and sat down in the empty seat across from mine. Once he did so, though, I lost all ability to concentrate. I was sure he'd come to me to get something off his chest. I felt compelled to close the periodical I'd been reading. As I made ready to go, K asked, in a fully composed voice, if I'd finished already. I told him it could wait till later. I returned the periodical, and we left the library together.

Wandering at will, we passed through Tatsuoka-chō to Ikenohata, then entered the park at Ueno. At this point, K suddenly broached the subject. Taking in the situation as a whole, it's quite clear that this was why he'd invited me out. However, he still had no idea where to go with his feelings. He turned to me and asked, in the vaguest of terms, what I thought. What he wanted to know was what I thought of his falling in love. In short, he sought my critique of his present state. This confirmed to me that he was far from his usual self. As I've often noted before, he was not one to bend his will to the whims of others. He was stronger than that. If he thought something right, he had the courage and grit to do it, on his own if need be. The affair with his foster family had impressed upon me the strength of his character. It should be no surprise then, that I regarded him now as changed.

I turned to K and asked him why he sought my opinion on this occasion. He replied, in an uncharacteristically disconsolate tone, that he was truly ashamed of his own weakness. He was in a quandary and had lost his way, he added, and saw no recourse but to turn to me for objective advice. I asked him, first off, what he meant by "losing his way." He explained that he wasn't sure whether to advance or withdraw. I immediately moved a step forward. Was he capable of withdrawal, I asked, if that were his chosen course. His words stuck in his throat. All he could say was that he found it unbearable. His anguish, in fact, was written on his face. Had the other party been anyone other than our young lady, I would have been moved to comfort him, to quench his pain with merciful words. If you'll allow me to say so, I believe I possess such noble compassion. In that moment, though, that is not who I was.

Chapter 41

I regarded K as though preparing for combat. All of me, my eyes, my heart, my body, everything that was mine, was directed at him fully. K was without sin and vulnerable. Perhaps vulnerable is not the right word. He was utterly and completely open and exposed. I could take from his hands the very plans to the stronghold housing his soul, and I could study those plans at leisure, in front of him in plain sight.

I'd found him wavering, lost between ideals and actuality, and I fixated now on taking him down with a telling blow. In an instant I'd set my sights. I turned to him anew with a solemn and steely air. It was tactical posturing, of course, but there was enough tension in my mood to mask all sense of absurdity or shame. I let loose first with, "Those not seeking betterment of the spirit are nothing but simpletons." These were the words K had spoken to me as the two of us traveled through Bōshū. I threw them back at him, in the same manner and in the same tone. This wasn't just retaliation. I'll confess that it was more. There was an undertone of cruelty. With these words, I sought to stamp out the spark of his affections.

K had been born to a Shinshū priest. However, his leanings from middle school on were hardly aligned with the tenets of his birth home. I'm no expert in doctrine, and I'll admit that I'm poorly qualified to comment on the subject, but nowhere were the differences clearer than with respect to the relationship between the sexes. K had always spoken of his "devotion." This term, as I understood it, implied abstinence. However, I'd learned from him over time, to my surprise, that it went much further. First and foremost, he believed firmly that all was subservient to "the way." All indulgences must be suppressed, and even an unconsummated desire would hinder one's progress. In those days when K had supported himself, he'd often shared with me his convictions. My mind being occupied with thoughts of the young lady, I'd contested his assertions with vigor. In return for my argument, he would give me a pitying look, though richer by far in contempt than in sympathy.

Given this shared history between us, the words, "Those not seeking betterment of the spirit are nothing but simpletons," were no doubt a slap in K's face. As I've stated before, though, it was not my intent to tear down that which he'd worked so hard to build up. On the contrary,

I wanted to see him to build it higher. Whether this led him to "the way," or whether it led him to nirvana did not concern me. I simply feared any abrupt swing in his worldview that would bring his interests into conflict with mine. In short, my words were purely self-serving.

"Those not seeking betterment of the spirit are nothing but simpletons."

I repeated these same words again, then watched to see their effect.

"A simpleton," he finally answered. "That's all that I am."

K came to a stop where he was. His eyes were cast downward. A chill ran through me. I feared I'd pushed him too far and braced myself for a backlash. However, I'd also noted the lack of any vitality in his voice. I wanted to read his eyes, but he didn't turn to face me. He slowly resumed walking.

Chapter 42

I walked along with K, but my heart hung back in shadow, waiting on this next words. Perhaps "lying in wait" is the better way to express it. In the state I was in, I wouldn't have put it past me to stab him from behind. At the same time, I did possess a conscience becoming of my upbringing. If someone, anyone, had whispered in my ear how mean I'd become, I'd likely have caught myself on the spot. If that someone had been K, I'd have certainly reddened for shame. But K was too true to rebuke me. He was too pure. He was too noble of character. All this in him that I should have respected, in my rage I used against him. I exploited his virtues to cut him down.

After a while, K spoke my name and turned to me. This time it was I who reflexively halted. Finally, I was able to look him in the eye. K was taller than me, so I was necessarily looking up. My wolf's heart, thus positioned, eyed the guileless sheep.

"Let's talk on this no further," he said. In both his eyes and his voice was an inexplicable sorrow. I could give no response. "Please, let's talk on this no further." This time he entreated me.

The answer I gave him was harsh. The wolf had spotted an opening and lunged in for the kill. "It wasn't I who started this, was it? It was you. If you want to stop, then fine, but you can't just mask it in silence. Are you prepared, in your heart, to truly let it go? And what of those tenets you've held so tightly? Where on earth are they now?"

K's stature seemed to diminish before me as I spoke. He was, as I've often noted, exceedingly set in his worldview. He was also, at the same time, a man of utmost integrity, and it upset him no end to be reproached for hypocrisy. As I watched him, I felt confident that my words had finally found their mark.

"Prepared?" he suddenly asked. "Prepared—why would I not be prepared?" he added before I could answer.

His words seemed meant for himself. He spoke as though in a daze.

We both fell silent and continued on toward the residence in Koishikawa. It was a comparatively calm and mild day, but it was winter nonetheless, and the park was deserted. When I looked back at the cedars, robbed of their verdure by harsh frosts, towering reddish-brown against the dusky sky, I felt an acute chill down my spine. We hurried on through the twilight, traversing Hongō Hill and descending into

Koishikawa valley toward the next hill beyond. By this point, my body was finally warming itself under my overcoat.

Due in part to our rapid pace, we hardly spoke the whole way back. Once at home and gathered at the table for dinner, Okusan asked what had kept us. I told her that K had invited me out and we'd walked in Ueno. Okusan expressed her surprise that we'd walked in the cold. Her daughter wanted to know what had drawn us to Ueno. I answered her that nothing had drawn us. We'd simply gone walking. K, who was never talkative to begin with, was even less so than usual. He hardly reacted to Okusan's questions or the daughter's laughter. He gulped down his food and was gone, retreating to his room while I remained at the table.

Chapter 43

In those days, we did not yet speak of "personal awakening" or "new take on life." It wasn't for lack of modern thinking, though, that K clung tight to his past and held his passions at bay. He'd simply invested too much. He'd lived thus far with singular purpose. His failure to run headlong after the object of his desire, therefore, could not be attributed to lack of ardor. However fierce his passions might burn, he could not be given to rash pursuit. Unless events should somehow tear him from his roots, he was compelled to hold his ground and respect the path he'd trodden. The only way he could honor his past was by holding firm to this same path. On top of this was his great penchant for obstinacy and perseverance. I felt that I possessed, in knowing his past and understanding his temperament, a window into his soul.

That evening after Ueno, I found myself comparatively at ease. After K retired to his room, I followed after and seated myself by his desk. I made a point of engaging him in idle talk. I could sense he was annoyed. I imagine my eyes held a glimmer of triumph, and I imagine my voice rang proud. After warming my hands over his hibachi for a while, I returned to my own room. K was my better in all things, but this time, I felt, it was I who held the winning hand.

Before long I was sound asleep. However, I woke abruptly to a voice calling my name. The fusuma was open, and I could see K's dark silhouette in the gap. His lamp was still burning, just as earlier in the evening. Suddenly aroused from the realm of sleep, I was too dazed to speak. I looked up at him blankly.

K asked if I was asleep. He was never one to retire early. I turned toward the dark shadow and asked in return if he needed anything. He replied that it was nothing in particular. He'd been up to use the toilet and was simply wondering whether I was still awake or had gone to bed. The light from his lamp fell on his backside, so I couldn't see his face or gauge his eyes. His voice, however, seemed fully at ease.

After a moment, K slid the fusuma closed. My room sank back into darkness. Preferring my dreams to the darkness, I again closed my eyes. The next moment it was morning. When I thought back on the night before, it all seemed strange. I wondered if I hadn't been dreaming. At breakfast, I asked K. He confirmed that he had indeed opened the fusuma and called my name. When I asked him why, he didn't provide a clear answer. He asked me then if I'd been out of sorts lately and not sleeping well. I found his question odd.

Both of our lectures began at the same time that day, so we left the house together. The incident of the previous evening had been bothering me all morning, so along the way I pressed him again. However, I still received no satisfactory explanation. I asked him if he needed to tell me something, perhaps on the matter of late. He replied emphatically that such was not the case. I sensed reproach in his tone. He was reminding me that we'd agreed to speak of it no further. In such situations, K was defiantly proud. As I remembered this, I suddenly reflected on his use of the word "prepared." This single word, to which I'd paid little heed before, began suddenly to exert a strange power in my mind.

Chapter 44

I knew very well that K was decisive by nature. It was clear to me too that on the matter at hand he was wavering. In short, my familiarity with the usual gave me confidence in discerning the exception. However, as I ruminated further on his use of "prepared," my confidence faded and before long was utterly shaken. I began to think that maybe there was no exception. I began to suspect that, deep within, he was embracing some decisive measure, a measure that would banish at once the entirety of his doubt, anguish, and agitation. As I considered the word "prepared" in this new light, I was left unsettled. I wish now that I'd stepped back from my agitation, just for a moment, for a second impartial take on what he truly meant. Regrettably, I was half blind. I could only think that K was "prepared" to make his move with respect to the daughter. He was prepared, I convinced myself, to act decisively in pursuit of his passion.

A voice in my heart told me it was now or never. In response, I began to steel my resolve. I had to take things in hand, before K did, and before he even caught wind. I waited in the wings for my chance. However, two days passed, and then three, with no chance presenting itself. I sought to engage Okusan when K and the daughter were both away. The days continued on, though, and if one was gone the other was there to impede me. There was never an opportune time. I was beside myself.

After a week, I could take it no longer and feigned illness. Okusan and her daughter, and even K himself, pressed me to get out of bed. I gave but cursory answers, and I stayed under my quilt till close to ten. I waited until K and the daughter were both gone, and the house was silent, and only then did I get out of bed. Okusan, on seeing me, asked first if I wasn't unwell. She advised me to get more rest and offered to bring a tray to my bedside. There was nothing physically wrong with me, and I had no intention now of going back to bed. I washed my face and took my meal in the hearth room as usual. Okusan sat on the other side of the long brazier and served me. Sitting there with bowl in hand, something between breakfast and lunch, my thoughts were fixed on how to state my case. As such, I can well imagine I did look a little unwell.

I finished eating and started a smoke. I didn't make to get up, so Okusan too was obliged to remain. She called the maidservant to clear away my dining tray. Then she added water to the iron kettle and wiped down the rim of the brazier, keeping me company as she did so. I asked if she had any particular plans for the day. She said she didn't, then asked in return why I'd wanted to know. I replied that there was a matter on which I'd hoped we could talk. She looked at me and asked what it was. She asked with a casual air, unaware of the gravity of my feelings, and I struggled a bit with how next to proceed.

Having no other recourse, I beat around the bush for a time before finally asking if K had said anything to her of late. "Regarding what?" she asked in return as though caught off guard. Before I could answer, she followed with a second question. "Did he say something to you?"

Chapter 45

"No," I replied. I had no intention of conveying K's confession to her. As soon as I spoke, though, I felt I was wrong in deceiving her. Having no other recourse, I restated my answer. I told her there was nothing in particular he'd asked me to convey, that my matter of concern was not about K. Accepting this, she waited on me to continue. There was now no going back. "Okusan, I'd like your daughter's hand," I said without further hesitation. This didn't seem to surprise her as much as I'd thought it would. Even so, she was momentarily speechless. She studied my face in silence. Having said what I'd said, I was in no position to fret over her scrutiny. "Please," I said, "I beseech you. Let me take her as my wife." Okusan, with her experience of years, was more composed than I was. "I don't see why not, but isn't this rather sudden?" she replied. "Sudden is what I want," I blurted back in return. My answer was met with a smile. "Are you sure you've thought this through?" she asked me again to gauge my resolve. I answered emphatically that however sudden my supplication might seem, my thought process was nothing if not deliberate.

Some degree of exchange followed, but I've forgotten now what was said. Okusan was not your typical female. She spoke decisively like a man, and this was a saving grace in situations such as this. "Very well then, you may take her," she said. "In fact, it's presumptuous of me to say you may take her. Please be good enough to take her. As you know, her situation is unfortunate, with her father no longer with us." She ended thus in entreating me.

Our discussion was simple and clear-cut. From start to finish, it lasted no more than fifteen minutes. Okusan brought forth no caveats. There was no need to consult with relations. It would suffice to notify them later. Her daughter's acceptance, she assured me, went without saying. On this point, as an educated man, I was more wont to stand on protocol. I wasn't concerned with relations, but I advised that it would be proper to discuss with her daughter and receive explicit agreement. Okusan replied that this was unnecessary. She was not committing to anything to which her daughter might object.

Back in my room, reflecting on how easily things had gone, it struck me as almost surreal. Doubts even entered my mind. Was all of this duly settled? At the same time, I knew that my future fortune, for the most part, had now been decided. I felt as though renewed to my core.

Around noon I went back to the hearth room and asked Okusan when she intended to tell her daughter. Okusan saw no urgency. As long as she herself knew, the matter was settled. At this point, Okusan struck me as the more masculine one of us, and I prepared to withdraw. As I did so, she stopped me. If I wished it to be soon, she would tell her daughter today when she returned home from her lessons. I told her I thought this best and then went back to my room. However, sitting there silently at my desk as the two of them talked in private, I decided on further reflection, would be too much to take. I put on my hat and headed out. At the bottom of the hill, I once again met the daughter. Not knowing what had transpired, she was surprised to see me. I removed my hat and greeted her. She asked with a curious look if I was better already. "I am better, much better," I answered before bearing off briskly toward Suidōbashi.

Chapter 46

I made my way through Sarugakuchō, came out on the boulevard at Jinbōchō, and then headed toward Ogawamachi. Usually, when I strolled these environs it was in search of used books, but on that particular day I felt no interest in hand-worn tomes. All the while I walked, my mind was back at the house. I relived my conversation of the morning with Okusan. Then I imagined the scene playing out between her and her daughter. These two sets of thoughts, in a sense, were the driving force of my feet. Then from time to time, unwittingly, I would stop in my tracks in the middle of the street. About now, I would think, Okusan must be talking to her daughter. Again later, I thought that they must by now have finished.

As I continued on, I crossed Mansei Bridge, ascended the hill at Myōjin, topped the Hongō Heights, descended Kiku Hill, and finally made my way down into the Koishikawa valley. The extent of my walk drew a circle through three districts, albeit a far from perfect one. All the while on this long walk, I gave hardly a thought to K. When I think back now and ask myself why, I have no answer. All I can say is that it still strikes me as odd. I can tell myself that I was simply overwrought by events at hand, but even at that my conscience should have intervened.

It was only after I returned home, when I slid open the latticework door and made my way from the entry hall to my own room, passing through K's room in the usual way, that my conscience reawakened. K was at his desk, reading as always. And as always, he raised his eyes from his book to regard me. However, he didn't give his standard greeting, asking if I had just now returned. Instead, he asked if I was better, and if I'd been out to see the doctor. In that moment, I wanted to prostrate myself before him and ask his forgiveness. The impulse to do so, at the time, was by no means lacking in intensity. Had the two of us stood alone in the wilderness, I'd surely have followed my conscience and apologized to him then and there. However, there were others in the house with us, and their presence served to hold me in check. Regrettably, I remained in check forevermore.

K and I were together again at dinner. K seemed lost in his own thoughts. Unaware, he in no way regarded me with suspicion. Okusan, also unaware, was in higher spirits than usual. I alone knew everything. My dinner went down like lead. On that occasion, the daughter didn't join us at the table as usual. When Okusan called her, she would only answer from the next room that she was coming. K seemed to find their exchange curious. He finally asked Okusan if something was amiss. Okusan, with a glance my way, answered that her daughter must be feeling abashed. K found this all the more curious, and proceeded to ask what had made her feel abashed. Okusan looked my way with a grin.

On my arrival at the table, I could surmise from Okusan's expression how things had gone. However, having her tell K, by way of explanation, with me there present, would have been excruciating. Okusan was not a woman to mince words, and I didn't put it past her to do so, so I sat there on pins and needles. Fortunately, K reverted to his previous reticence. Okusan, though in a cheerful mood, in the end refrained from offering up the discussion I so dreaded. I returned to my room with a sigh of relief. However, I was compelled to wrestle with the problem of how to deal with K going forward. In my heart, I conjured up myriad justifications to defend myself before him, but none seemed adequate. Spineless as I was, I grew loath to explain myself at all.

Chapter 47

I spent several days in this state. Needless to say, my breast was heavy the whole while with apprehension. I knew full well that I must, somehow, make amends with K. To make matters worse, Okusan's manner and the daughter's comportment were a constant prod at my conscience. There was no telling when Okusan, who lacked the reserve typical of women, might spill all to K at the dinner table. It was also quite possible that the daughter's bearing and behavior, which now to me seemed noticeably changed, could serve to sow seeds of suspicion in his mind. I had to disclose to him, somehow, my new connection to this family. This struck me, however, in light of my own moral shortcomings, as the hardest thing in the world to do.

I thought about asking Okusan to find some occasion to tell him. This would, of course, be in my absence. The facts of the matter, though, even if conveyed indirectly rather than directly, were no less shameful. Furthermore, whatever rationalization I might scheme up, Okusan was unlikely to convey it to K without due explanation on my part. To come clean, in order to secure her assistance, would mean exposing my own shortcomings to the young lady of my affections, as well as to my future mother-in-law. In my mind, I saw this as an indelible stain on my future credibility. The prospect of losing even an iota of trust in the eyes of my bride, before we were yet wed, was utterly abhorrent.

In short, I was a wretch who'd set out on the narrow path of virtue, lost his footing, and fallen into the mire. Either that, or I was an underhanded schemer. This conundrum, though, to this point, was a secret shared by myself and heaven alone. I stood in predicament. The only way to regain my footing and retake the narrow path was through confession of my misdeeds to those around me. I was loath to confess. At the same time, I was loath to remain in the mire. I was paralyzed, wedged between a rock and a hard place.

Five or six days later, Okusan suddenly asked me if I'd informed K of the matter at hand. I told her I hadn't. She then asked, rather scoldingly, why it was that I hadn't. I tensed up as she queried me. Her next words were a shock. I remember them still to this day.

"That would explain his odd reaction when I mentioned it. The fault lies as much with you as with me. How could you leave him in the dark when you've always been so close?"

I asked her what he'd said when she told him. She replied that he hadn't said much in particular. However, I couldn't refrain from pressing her further. She saw no reason, of course, to keep anything from me. Still saying it was nothing of import, she related the scene in detail.

Based on all that she told me, K had managed to keep himself fully composed. This despite the fact that it must have been quite a blow to him. He'd given only a curt response on learning of the new relationship between myself and the daughter. However, when Okusan pointed out that he should be happy for us, he had allowed himself a smile and congratulated her. Then he'd risen to take his leave. Before pushing aside the hearth room shōji on his way out, he'd turned back to Okusan and asked when the wedding would be.

As she described it, he then added that he would like to offer us a congratulatory gift, but lacked the means to do so. As I sat before Okusan and heard this, an ache arose in my heart.

Chapter 48

By my reckoning, it had been two full days since Okusan's talk with K. During this time, K's behavior toward me had betrayed nothing, and I'd been utterly unaware. On the outside, at least, his emotions were fully in check, and I had to admire his forbearance. When I thought about K in comparison to myself, he was without doubt the superior man. I may have outmaneuvered him as a rival, but as a human being I was beaten. This feeling swelled in my breast. Thinking how K must despise me, my face flushed red for shame. My pride, however, prevented me still from throwing myself at his feet.

Torn between action and inaction, I decided, at any rate, to give it another day. This was Saturday evening. That very night, however, K died by his own hand. Even today, I shudder to recall the scene. I always slept with my head toward the east. On that night only, for whatever reason, I laid out my bedding with my head to the west. Perhaps there was some connection. I woke suddenly to a cold draft crossing my pillow. I looked and saw that the fusuma, partitioning K's room from mine, stood open, just as it had on that previous night. Unlike that night, though, K's silhouette did not fill the frame. Sensing something amiss, I propped myself onto my elbows and took a look into K's room. His lamp was burning dimly. His bedding had been laid out. However, his quilt had been pushed into a pile at the foot of it. K himself was lying prone with his face turned away.

I called out to him. There was no answer. I called again and asked if he wasn't well. There was no reaction. I immediately rose to my feet and advanced as far as the threshold. From there, I surveyed his room in the dim light of the lamp.

The initial sensation I received was much like that of the moment of his confession. With one sweep of his room, my eyes turned to glass and lost their capacity for movement. I stood there frozen. Paralysis gripped and then released me, like a gust of passing wind. As it swept on its way, I knew that all was lost. A dark shadow, never to be lifted, spilled across my future days. In an instant it cast its pall, with terrifying force, over the entirety of my existence. My body began to tremble.

Even so, I couldn't forget my own preservation. A letter on the desk immediately caught my eye. As expected, it bore my name. Feverishly, I removed the seal. Inside, however, were none of the words

I'd anticipated. What I'd anticipated were stinging words of censure, expounding on my sins. Such words, I'd feared, would utterly damn me in Okusan's or her daughter's eyes. On quick inspection, I knew I'd been spared. (I'd been spared, of course, only in the eyes of society, but the eyes of society, in this circumstance, dominated my thoughts.)

The contents of the letter were simple. They tended toward the abstract. K, by weakness of character, saw no hope of realizing his ambitions, and was therefore ending his life. After that, he'd added his thanks to me, in very plain language, for the assistance I'd provided. As one last act of assistance, he asked that I handle his affairs after his passing. The distress he would be causing Okusan was unpardonable, and I should by all means apologize on his behalf. He requested that I notify his kin back home. He touched briefly on all he needed to touch on, but there was no mention of the daughter. It occurred to me, after reading the letter through, that he'd purposefully avoided her. What pained me most of all, though, was the final phrase. He'd appended it, it appeared, to exhaust the ink in his pen. He should have, he wrote, died sooner. To what avail, he wondered, had he lived so long.

With trembling hands I rerolled and resealed the letter. I made a point of placing it back on the desk for all to see. I turned then, and for the first time noticed the splash of blood on the fusuma.

Chapter 49

Impulsively, I cupped K's head in both hands and lifted it a little. I sought to regard his face in death. He was lying prone, and after one quick look at his face from below, I immediately withdrew my hands. It was more than just fear. I was shocked by the weight of his head. From above, I gazed for some time at the cold ears I'd just touched, and at the thick, close-cropped hair that appeared no different than usual. I felt no urge to weep. I felt only terror. The terror I felt, though, was more than the simple terror of my senses reacting to the scene before me. It was a profound terror, a terror of the Fates, embodied here in this friend so suddenly cold.

Lacking the wit to do otherwise, I returned to my own room. I began to pace its length and breadth. My mind commanded me to keep moving, even if for naught. I thought that I must, somehow, do something. At the same time, I knew there was nothing to be done. I couldn't refrain from circling the room. I paced like a bear in a cage.

More than once, I thought to go in and wake Okusan. I was restrained, though, by the thought that the scene was too dreadful for her. A firm desire to spare the ladies, particularly the daughter, from the shock of this all, held me in check. So reasoning, I thus resumed my pacing.

During this time, I lit my lamp. Then, occasionally, I would glance at the clock. Never have I seen anything move with such reluctance as the hands of that clock. I don't know exactly when I woke, but I know it was close to daybreak. As I continued to pace, anxiously awaiting the dawn, my thoughts were plagued by illusions and fears of endless night.

We typically rose before seven. Classes often started at eight, and if we woke any later we wouldn't make it on time. With this in mind, the maidservant was always up around six. On that day, however, it was not yet six when I went to wake her. As I did so, Okusan reminded me it was Sunday. She'd woken to the sound of my steps. I asked Okusan, since she was already up, if she couldn't come to my room for a moment. She threw her half coat on over her nightgown and followed me back. As soon as we were in the room, I immediately slid shut the fusuma that stood open in the partition between K's room and mine. I then informed Okusan, in a hushed voice, that something terrible had happened. She asked what it was. With my chin I gestured toward the next room. "Please brace yourself," I started. The color drained from her face. "Okusan, K has taken his own life," I continued. She froze in place and gazed at my face in silence. In that moment, I suddenly put my hands to the floor, lowered my head, and apologized. "I'm so sorry. This is my fault. I've brought this all on you and your daughter." Until I'd seen her reaction, I'd had no intention of voicing such words. However, the look on her face had made me forget myself. This was the apology I could never now make to K, delivered instead, of necessity, to Okusan and her daughter. In short, my better nature overcame me, broke through my façade, and brought forth words of repentance. Fortunately for my sake, Okusan did not read these words so deeply. "No one could have known. You mustn't blame yourself," she spoke to console me. Her face was still without color. Shock and fear had seized its sinews and pulled them taught, etching deep lines.

Chapter 50

Though I hated to do it, I rose again and re-opened the door I'd just closed. K's lamp, it seems, had exhausted its oil, and his room lay in total darkness. I went back for my own lamp, advanced to the threshold, then turned round to Okusan. From behind me, remaining in my shadow, she peered into the small room. She made no move to enter. From where she stood, she asked that I open the storm shutters.

From there on, Okusan showed the mettle of an army widow, taking command of the situation. I made the rounds, first to the doctor and then to the police. However, I did so under Okusan's instruction. Until all such formalities were concluded, she allowed no one into the room.

K had cut his carotid artery with a small knife and died instantly. Apart from this, his body bore no wound. I learned that the blood I'd seen on the shōji, in that dim light of a dream, had gushed forth from his neck. In the full light of day, I looked again and saw clearly the stains it had left. In so doing, I was struck by the force with which blood courses through the body.

Okusan and I did our best to clean K's room. Fortunately, most of his blood had been captured by his bedding. The tatami mats were only lightly soiled and easily washed. We moved his body into my room and laid it out in a natural sleeping position. I then went out to wire his family.

When I returned, incense was burning at K's bedside. The room hung heavy with spiritual vapors, and I saw the two women seated in their midst. This was the first time since the prior evening that I'd seen the daughter. She was weeping. Okusan's eyes, too, were red with traces of tears. I'd held back my own tears thus far, but finally, in that moment, I indulged myself in sadness. Melancholy welled in my breast, and I can't overstate the comfort it brought. My heart, which had been gripped so tightly by anguish and fear, received in that moment a first drop of cool relief.

Without speaking, I seated myself next to the ladies. Okusan suggested I offer a stick of incense. I offered my incense and remained seated, still saying nothing. The daughter did not address me. She occasionally exchanged a word or two with her mother, but only concerning tasks at hand. She was not yet, it seemed, ready to talk of K and the times we had had. Inwardly, I was relieved to have spared her the frightful scene of the night prior. To show such horror to one so young and so beautiful, I'd feared, would only risk marring her grace. Even at the height of my own terror, when my hair had stood on end, this thought had governed my actions. The idea of exposing her to the same terror was, to me, no less unsavory than the thought of thrashing a blameless flower to shreds.

K's father and brother arrived from the country, and I shared with them my recommendation regarding his remains. K and I had often strolled Zōshigaya. K was very much taken with the place. I remembered telling him, half in jest, that if he liked it so much then I'd see he was buried there. I wondered if there was really any virtue now in doing as I'd promised. I did desire, though, to kneel each month at his grave, for as long as I might live, and express anew my regret. Perhaps out of obligation to me, as I'd looked after K while they had not, his father and brother readily acquiesced.

Chapter 51

I was asked by one of K's friends, as we made our way back from the funeral, why I thought he had killed himself. Since that fateful night, I'd been tormented repeatedly by this question. From Okusan, to her daughter, to K's father and brother arriving from the country, to acquaintances who were notified, to newspaper reporters with no connection whatsoever to K, none failed to pose this question. And each time it was posed, the question stung at my conscience. I could hear behind the question a voice, hounding me, telling me to confess my wrongdoing.

The answer I gave to all was the same. I simply related what K had written in the letter he'd left me. I offered up nothing more. K's friend, who on the way back from the funeral had posed the same question and received my standard answer, took a newspaper from his pocket to show me. He pointed out a passage and, still walking, I read where directed. It reported how K, estranged from his family, had fallen into misanthropic despair and ended his life. Without comment, I refolded the paper and returned it to the friend. According to other papers, he informed me, it was mental instability that led to K's suicide. I'd been too busy to read the papers and had no idea what had been reported. However, there wasn't a moment when it didn't weigh on my mind. What I feared most of all was anything enmeshing the other members of the household. Even the mention of the daughter's name, in my mind, was unbearable. I asked the friend if anything else had been reported. Other than those two story lines, he replied, he hadn't seen anything else.

Shortly thereafter we moved to our present home. Both Okusan and her daughter were averse to remaining, and reliving the memory of that evening, night after night, was more than I could face. We talked it over and decided to leave.

Two months after we moved, I graduated from the university as anticipated. Half a year after my graduation, the daughter and I were finally wed. From the outside, all was progressing as hoped, and one would have to conclude that these were happy times. Okusan and her daughter seemed duly content. And I too was content. However, to my contentment was tethered a dark shadow. I saw my contentment as a powder train, burning its way toward some final, sorrowful fate.

After we were married, the daughter—we were married now, so I should rather say my wife—my wife, for whatever reason, suggested that we visit K's gravesite together. My immediate reaction was visceral aversion. Why, I asked, had she suddenly thought to do so. To have us both visit together, she replied, would surely be pleasing to K. I gazed back intently at her face. She had no idea why, and she asked me what was wrong. Only then was I aware of what I was doing.

I took my wife to Zōshigaya as she wished. I ladled water onto K's gravestone to cleanse it. She set out incense and flowers. The two of us inclined our heads and pressed our hands together in prayer. My wife, I expect, was telling K of our life together, thinking how pleased he would be. In my own heart, all I could do was reproach myself over and over.

My wife ran her hand over K's gravestone and noted how splendid it was. It wasn't much of a stone, but I'd gone to the stone seller and picked it out myself, so for this reason, I expect, she made a point of praising it. Conjuring in my mind this new gravestone, my new wife, and the newly interred bones lying under the earth, I couldn't but feel mocked by the Fates. After that day, I decided I would never again visit K's grave with my wife.

Chapter 52

My sentiments regarding my deceased friend were never to change. Truth be told, I had feared such an outcome. It's fair to say that even at my wedding, which I'd looked forward to for so long, I was riddled with anxiety. As humans, however, we're not blessed with the luxury of foresight, and I had hoped that, perhaps, marriage would serve as a turning point, renewing my spirit and setting my life on a new course. As a husband, though, looking daily on his wife, my hopes were short-lived, easily broken by harsh realities. During our times together, K would appear without warning and haunt my mind. My wife, as I came to see things, was the bond between K and myself, securely grasping both of our fates. I could find no fault with her otherwise, but this one facet was enough to push me away. A woman soon senses such things. But what she sensed, she could not explain. She pressed me at times for an answer. She wanted to know why I felt as I did, if there was something she'd done to displease me. At times I was able to disarm her with a smile. At other times, though, her patience reached its limit. In the end, I would suffer her reproaches. "Why do you hate me so?" she would say, or "There has to be something you're hiding."

There were many times I resolved to confide in her, to tell her all. However, whenever I found myself on the verge of doing so, other forces would intervene and hold me back. You know me well, so I believe this goes without saying, but I state it here for the sake of completeness. I was never one to put on airs with my wife. Had I approached her in good faith with words of penitence, the same way I approached my deceased friend, I know that she would have embraced me, shedding tears of joy, and forgiven my indiscretions. It was certainly not a calculated self-interest that kept me from doing so. It was rather the thought of tarnishing her past, of smearing it with a dark stain, that I couldn't accept. Please understand how loath I was to let something so pure be defiled with stains of black.

A year passed, and thoughts of K continued to grip my soul, fueling a constant anxiety. To dispel this anxiety, I immersed myself in my books. With great intensity of purpose, I applied myself to my studies. I looked toward a future where I would share the fruits of my work with the world. As it turned out, however, my concocted goals, and my visions of renown, were nothing but hollow façades. Dissatisfied, I lost my drive and turned away from my work. I sat with folded arms, watching the world go by.

My wife attributed my let-down to lack of immediate necessity. Her family was well enough off that she and her mother could get along without outside income, and my own circumstances did not compel me to seek an occupation, so it was only natural she should see things so. I do have a tendency to indulge myself. However, the real reason behind my withdrawal lay entirely elsewhere. After my uncle deceived me, I'd lost my faith in the world. While deeming the world flawed, I'd declared myself to be true. I'd held the conviction that, be the world as it may, I could hone in myself a shining example of humanity. That conviction was laid waste by K. The sudden realization that I was no better than my uncle was devastating. My disenchantment with others extended now to myself, rendering all effort futile.

Chapter 53

Having failed to lose myself in my books, I tried for a time to forget myself by drowning my soul in saké. I can't say I'm given to drink. However, I can drink when I want to, and with enough drink, I thought, I could quell the ache in my heart. Such shallow expedient, over time, only furthered my sense of misanthropy. In the height of drunken stupor, I would suddenly come to myself. I would feel a fool, going to lengths to delude myself so. With a shudder, my eyes and my heart would both snap to sobriety. There were also times when no amount of drink could push the world away, when all I did was depress myself. Furthermore, every pleasurable moment I finessed from the bottle was paid back in full with subsequent gloom. The people I cherished most, my wife and her mother, bore witness to this. They could only judge me, of course, on the basis of that which they knew.

My wife's mother, it seems, sometimes voiced her disapproval. My wife kept this from me. However, she couldn't always refrain from reproaching me of her own accord. Even when she reproached me, she was not harsh. Only rarely did her words ever rile me. She would often entreat me to tell her honestly what she'd done to displease me. She would caution me, for the sake of my own future, to not drink so. Sometimes she would weep and tell me I'd changed. That was fair, but then she would add, "You wouldn't be like this if K were alive." At times I acknowledged that perhaps this was so. However, the meaning in my acknowledgement and the meaning she took from it were a world apart. Inwardly, this saddened me. Even so, I was not inclined to explain myself.

I did, at times, apologize to my wife. This would be in the morning, after a night of drinking heavily and arriving home late. She would sometimes respond with a smile. At other times I was met with silence. Once in a while she'd break down and cry. In any case, I was left with a hollow feeling. My apologies, you could say, were as much to myself as my wife. In the end, I eased up on the drink. Truth be told, it was my own sense of revulsion, more than my wife's admonishments, that finally led me to do so.

I eased up on the drink but still felt no desire to work. With nothing else to do, I turned back to my books. Whatever I read, however, I would lay aside and forget. My wife asked me, on multiple occasions, to what end I studied. I would force a smile in return. Deep down, though, it pained me greatly to think that the one person in this world whom I knew and trusted did not understand me. Worse yet, the solution was close at hand. Only my courage to invoke it was lacking. I was utterly alone. I often felt I'd been cut adrift, apart from the world, fated to solitude.

All during this time, my thoughts returned, again and again, to K and his death. For some time, based on simple and direct observation, the single word "love" had been fixed in my head. K must have certainly, I'd concluded, died of a broken heart. However, with the gradual passage of time and the clarity of steadier thought, I began to see it wasn't so simple. The clash of reality and ideals—that too was inadequate. I finally began to suspect that K, just like myself, had felt himself utterly alone in the world and, with no other recourse, had acted. A shudder ran down my spine. From this point on, a foreboding that I was following in K's footsteps would occasionally chill my breast, sweeping through like a draft of cold of air.

Chapter 54

Time went by, and my mother-in-law fell ill. The doctor examined her and told us there was nothing he could do. I spared no effort in providing for her care. I did this for her sake and for the sake of the wife whom I loved. But more than that, I did it for the sake of humanity. Up to that point I had longed greatly to engage with the world. It was only lack of capacity to do so, I believe, that left me an idler. I'd become isolated, and this was the first time I found myself taking initiative, albeit in small measure, for the greater good. I can't deny that I was possessed, in some sense, by a desire for atonement.

My mother-in-law passed away. My wife and I were left alone, just the two of us. My wife turned to me and told me I was now the only person in this world on whom she could depend. I couldn't even depend on myself, and when she looked at me so, I lost my composure. My mind was overcome with pity. I told her she was a terribly unfortunate woman. She asked my why. She didn't understand me, and I couldn't explain myself. She started to weep. She reproached me, telling me it was only my distorted notions of her that led me to say such things.

After the loss of her mother, I treated my wife with utmost kindness. I did this not only out of love. There was a broader context to my kindness, transcending the individual. Just as in caring for her mother, my heart again was stirred. My wife seemed content. Cast across her contentment, though, was the faintest of shadows, testimony to the distance between us. Even had I opened my heart to her, though, I'm not sure I could have vanquished this shadow. I believe that women, more so than men, when affections come their way are wont to find pleasure in romance, in intrigue. Affections born of obligation, or service to some greater good, are less alluring.

On one occasion, my wife wondered aloud whether a man's heart and a woman's heart could never truly join together as one. I answered vaguely that perhaps, in the case of young lovers, it was possible. She seemed to be reflecting on her past. Finally, she allowed from her lips the faintest of sighs.

Starting in those days, a dreadful shadow would sometimes flicker across my breast. At first it was something external, assailing me from without. It caught me by surprise. It horrified me. However, with the passing of time my heart grew to accept these flickers of dread. In the end, I came to regard them as part of myself, with me from the moment of my birth and dormant till now in the depths of my soul. This feeling, whenever it struck, made me wonder if I wasn't losing my mind. I had no intention, though, of having my head checked. Neither by a doctor, nor by anyone else.

I felt profoundly the flaws of humankind. It was this feeling that led me monthly to K's grave. It was this feeling too that compelled me to care so for my wife's ailing mother. And it was this feeling that commanded me to approach my wife with tenderness. Because of this feeling, there were even moments I wished for passersby, people unknown to me, to take up the whip and scourge me. As my thoughts progressed further, I felt that it was I, not others, who should take up the whip and scourge myself. Next came the notion that scourging would never do. I had to destroy myself. Having no other recourse, I resolved going forward to live as though I were dead.

How many years have passed since that time? My wife and I have continued on quietly together. By no measure have we been unhappy. We've found our contentment. However, this one part of me, the one part I can never change, has always darkened her world. When I think on this, I can't help but feel I've wronged her.

Chapter 55

This heart of mine, resolved to live as though dead, was sometimes stirred to life by outside influences. However, at the slightest thought of any initiative on my part, a dreadful force, appearing from who knows where, would seize my heart and pin it in place. This force, holding me tightly in its grasp, would berate me, telling me I was fit for nothing. Its rebuke was enough to instantly sap my will. In time, I would again try to rise, only to again be suppressed. I yelled in anger through clenched teeth, demanding to know by what right it held me in check. I was mocked in return by a chilling voice, reminding me that I already knew full well. My will again deserted me.

You should understand that even as we continued on in our quiet life, free from vicissitudes and complications, a bitter battle raged within me. For every time I upset my wife by letting it surface, I'd already upset myself a hundred times over. I realized, when I could no longer endure my personal prison, and when I knew I could never break out, that of the options before me, ending my life was the only practicable choice. Don't let this shock you. That mysterious force, the force that gripped my heart and blocked my every endeavor, held open to me the path to my death. I could remain still, but if I chose to move, even a little, there was only this single path.

Living till now, I've been tempted multiple times to follow this path of least resistance, this path which fate has laid out before me. On each such occasion, though, it was consideration for my wife that held me back. And I lack the temerity, of course, to take her with me. To one like myself, afraid to even open his heart, the mere thought of sacrificing my wife to my own fate, of cutting short her life by violent means, was enough to leave me shuddering. Just as my fate is my own, my wife too has a life that is hers. I couldn't but conclude that to feed the two of us, bundled together, to the same fire, would be tragically unjust.

At the same time, the thought of my wife left alone after my passing was equally unacceptable. She'd turned to me after her mother's death and told me I was the only one in the world now on whom she could depend. This memory was ingrained in the depths of my being. I thus remained ever indecisive. There were times when, seeing my wife's face, I was grateful not to have acted. I would pull back from the edge for a while. Then I would sense my wife regarding me, from time to time, with an unfulfilled look in her eyes.

Please understand that this is the way I lived. From our first meeting in Kamakura, to that day we strolled the outskirts of town, my sentiments were by and large the same. A dark shadow has stalked me all of my days. Only for the sake of my wife have I walked so long through this world. It was the same when you graduated and departed for home. When I promised I'd see you again in September, I was not insincere. I fully intended to see you. If autumn passed and winter came, and even if winter passed, I was certain I'd see you again.

Then, at the height of summer, His Majesty, the Meiji Emperor, passed away. I sensed that my time, along with this emperor, had come and gone. A feeling struck me that men like myself, having passed our days in the reign of Meiji, had no business living beyond it. We'd become, as it were, obsolete. I said as much to my wife. She smiled, brushing away my words. Then suddenly, for whatever reason, she added in jest that I could always honor my lord through ritual suicide, accompanying him to the grave.

Chapter 56

I'd hardly remembered there was such a term as "ritual suicide." It's not something one hears with any frequency anymore, and I seemed to have left it to decay from disuse in the bottom of my mind. When my wife's jest brought it back to the surface, I turned to her and replied that if I were to commit ritual suicide, it would be in honor of the era of Meiji, in honor of the spirit of a bygone age. My reply, of course, was likewise in jest, but I also felt that I'd gleaned new meaning from an archaic and disused term.

Another month went by. On the night of the Imperial Funeral, sitting in my study as usual, I listed to the sounding of the cannon. It seemed to say, with resounding finality, that the days of Meiji were forever gone. It was telling us too, as I thought on it later, that General Nogi had left us forever. When the extra edition of the paper arrived and I read of events, I instinctively repeated the words "ritual suicide" to my wife.

I read in the paper what General Nogi had written before his death. Since losing his banner in the Satsuma Rebellion, he'd wished to die by way of atonement. When I read these words, I reflexively put my fingers to work, counting out the years he'd lived with this wish. The Satsuma Rebellion had occurred during the tenth year of the Meiji reign, so thirty five years had passed from then until now. General Nogi, it seems, had for thirty five years waited for the right time to die. I wondered, for such a man, which was the greater anguish, those thirty five years of life or the instant of death when the dagger pierced his flesh.

It was several days later that I finally resolved to end my own life. Just as General Nogi's motives for dying were not fully known to me, my own reasons for dying may well be unclear to you. If that is the case, I expect it can't be helped. The passing of time puts distance between us. Or perhaps it's better said that we each enter this world with our own unique dispositions. I've tried through this narrative, to the best of my ability, to reveal to you my own peculiar self.

I'll be leaving my wife behind. It comforts me to know that I'm leaving her financially secure. I have no desire to expose her to anything horrific. I intend in dying to spare her the sight of blood. Unbeknownst to her, I'll slip silently from this world. After I'm dead, I'd like her to imagine I simply passed on without warning. If she believes I lost my senses, then that too is acceptable.

Ten days have passed since I decided to end my life. Please appreciate that the greater part of that time has gone into laying out my past for you on these pages. My initial thought was to talk with you face to face. However, once I started writing, I was soon satisfied that this is the better way to candidly set forth my life. I didn't approach this task lightly. My past, the events that made me who I am, is part of the human story, and a part that no one else can tell. I believe that these efforts, to leave for posterity an honest accounting of my life, will not be in vain, but will serve both you and others in shedding light on the human condition. I was told the other day how Watanabe Kazan pushed off the hour of his death by a week in order to finish his painting "Kantan." Some might dismiss this as vain effort, but there's no doubt the man had his reasons, some pull on his heart that allowed him to do no less. My own efforts are motivated by much more than just my promise to you. It's largely my own longing that spurs me on.

That longing, however, has now been duly quenched. I've done what I needed to do. By the time this letter reaches you, I'll be gone from this world. I'll have already passed away. My wife left ten days ago for her aunt's residence in Shibuya. Her aunt is ill and in need of assistance, and I encouraged her to go. I've written the greater part of this in her absence. On the occasions she's returned home, I've concealed it from her.

I offer this past of mine, unadulterated, to all who might seek to know it. However, you must accept that my wife is the sole exception. She's never to know these things. My sole request is for her memories of me to remain as they are, largely untarnished. Even after my death, for as long as she lives, you're to seal these revelations in your heart, as secrets of mine entrusted to you alone.

A Note About the Author

Natsume Sōseki (1867–1916) was a Japanese novelist. Born in Babashita, a town in the Edo region of Ushigome, Sōseki was the youngest of six children. Due to financial hardship, he was adopted by a childless couple who raised him from 1868 until their divorce eight years later, at which point Sōseki returned to his biological family. Educated in Tokyo, he took an interest in literature and went on to study English and Chinese Classics while at the Tokyo Imperial University. He started his career as a poet, publishing haiku with the help of his friend and fellow-writer Masaoka Shiki. In 1895, he found work as a teacher at a middle school in Shikoku, which would serve as inspiration for his popular novel *Botchan* (1906). In 1900, Sōseki was sent by the Japanese government to study at University College London. Later described as "the most unpleasant years in [his] life," Sōseki's time in London introduced him to British culture and earned him a position as a professor of English literature back in Tokyo. Recognized for such novels as *Sanshirō* (1908) and *Kokoro* (1914), Sōseki was a visionary artist whose deep commitment to the life of humanity has earned him praise from such figures as Haruki Murakami, who named Sōseki as his favorite writer.

A Note from the Publisher

Spanning many genres, from non-fiction essays to literature classics to children's books and lyric poetry, Mint Edition books showcase the master works of our time in a modern new package. The text is freshly typeset, is clean and easy to read, and features a new note about the author in each volume. Many books also include exclusive new introductory material. Every book boasts a striking new cover, which makes it as appropriate for collecting as it is for gift giving. Mint Edition books are only printed when a reader orders them, so natural resources are not wasted. We're proud that our books are never manufactured in excess and exist only in the exact quantity they need to be read and enjoyed. To learn more and view our library, go to minteditionbooks.com

bookfinity & MINT EDITIONS

Enjoy more of your favorite classics with Bookfinity,
a new search and discovery experience for readers.
With Bookfinity, you can discover more vintage
literature for your collection, find your Reader Type,
track books you've read or want to read,
and add reviews to your favorite books.
Visit www.bookfinity.com, and click on
Take the Quiz to get started.

Don't forget to follow us
@bookfinityofficial and @mint_editions

www.ingramcontent.com/pod-product-compliance
Ingram Content Group UK Ltd.
Pitfield, Milton Keynes, MK11 3LW, UK
UKHW021838140426
5217IPUK00022B/1504